THE TRAIL BOSS

THE TRAIL BOSS

WALTER GANN

CUTTING EDGE

ISBN-13: 978-1-954840-39-3

Published by
Cutting Edge Books
PO Box 8212
Calabasas, CA 91372
www.cuttingedgebooks.com

TABLE OF CONTENTS

THE TRAIL BOSS

CHAPTER ONE

IN A THICKET OF CHAPARRAL

Gloom folded over the cattle range in western Texas. Dark clouds rolled low and sifted out a misty rain which a north wind whipped in waves across barren hills and through leafless trees and brush. Raindrops crystallized into a raspy ice-crust as they lodged upon objects exposed to the cold wind. Small bunches of cattle loomed up like specters among the milky shadows. With lowered heads and tails dragging, they slish-sloshed along and faded from sight into the soppy fog as they drifted before the storm.

Bill Sanders leaned forward and bent his head into the wind, using his hat brim as a shield for his face against the slashing raindrops. He pulled his slicker tight around his body and shivered at the increasing wet and chill. On he rode, unmindful that almost within a stone's throw a life-and-death struggle was going on.

In a thicket of chaparral brush under the shelter of a low-breaking hill, Sancho, the calf, was born. Strangled gasps and weakly twitching eyelashes were the only evidence of life, and a pain-racked mother regarded him with uncertainty.

While her calf lay stretched helplessly among the ice-covered grass tufts, motherly instinct overcame pain and weakness and she took the first steps to revive a sinking spark of life, by nosing him around and licking his body in a rough massage. A courageous little heart responded and pumped life blood into flabby lung cells which drew in the first breath of air.

The line of his ancestors could be traced to the wild mountain cattle of ancient Spain. It was only a short step across the Atlantic to old San Antonio, where they were brought by the sport-loving *conquistadores*. Three centuries of propagation followed, until they settled into their natural place in history and tradition as the Texas Longhorn.

Now, with his blood in circulation, the calf rallied to fight for existence. His kind had never enjoyed the comfort and shelter of a barn lot with its bed of fragrant hay. Their only scheme of living was to fight — fight against three principal antagonists: the weather, wild animals, and men.

His only shelter now was the scattering limbs of a chaparral bush weighted down with glittering icicles through which sifted cold rain and chilling wind. His only bed was the soggy ground matted over with frozen grass blades, and his only protection against vicious animals was that of a jealous mother who stood over him and offered encouragement with her soft *m-m-m-m*.

A dull ache pulled at his insides, urging him to secure food. After many heart-breaking trials to gain a footing, his efforts were at last rewarded. He nosed around under his mother's side until his little jaws clamped upon one of her well-filled teats, and the warm milk flowed down his throat. He closed his eyes and his body quivered at the taste of food, and one obstacle in his life was overcome.

While he had won his first battle for existence, there were still many things beyond his comprehension. He had no way of knowing that in the world three human beings were eventually to come in contact with him, and that he was to be a strong influence in shaping their destiny.

First, there was Bill Sanders the cowboy, who had unconsciously passed him by during the lowest ebb of his struggle. Two hundred miles to the east was bright-eyed, eighteen-year-old Virginia Lowe eagerly looking forward to a visit with relatives, out in the wild cattle country. And something like three hundred miles southeast from where the calf stood arose the massive walls of an institution where men are sometimes sent for stealing other people's cattle. Inside those walls, serving out the tail end of his prison sentence, was an unrepentant desperado by the name of Ben Harte. He was also looking to the near future with eagerness. Years of brooding had created a scheme which he thought would furnish him an easy living from the earnings of other people.

Dawn next morning was cold and clear, but a glowing sun quickly softened the weather to normal spring temperature. That day the mother moved back toward the hills as far as her young calf could travel. The next day she moved still further, and by easy stages they arrived upon a wide plateau flanked by a rim of high ridges, where grass was plentiful. During these short journeys they encountered many other cows and their newborn calves. For common protection against predatory animals they held together in loosely formed bands.

After two weeks of uneventful life in which he did nothing but eat and sleep and play, his mother started out with him on a foraging expedition of their own. He had now reached the age in life when he should learn many things for himself.

Out over rocky hills and through brushy valleys she led him, teaching as they went along. She let him find out for himself the painful folly of butting around in a clump of bushes that harbored a nest of yellow-jackets, but she would relay a sharp warning to him at the buzz of a coiled rattlesnake, and would shake her head and throw her horns around in a threatening motion at the smell or sight of a prowling wolf.

A notorious killer wolf had traveled far in his flight before irate ranchmen. He succeeded in throwing the pursuers off his track, but safety was bought at the price of exhaustion. He had rested long, and now an aching hunger drove him from his hiding-place in search of food.

The smell of tainted meat from the carcass of a dead animal assailed his nostrils, but he put the temptation aside. That kind of food would not do for him. He had tried eating dead meat before, and as a reminder of his folly he could recall the painful experience of having to gnaw off three front toes and leave them clamped in the jaws of a steel trap. Instinct and learning had taught him that no traps could be hidden around a loose, live animal. Therefore he started out to hunt down and kill his own meat.

He had not traveled far with his nostrils tipped aloft until he caught the smell of a young calf. Instantly alert, he followed the scented breeze to where the calf lay sleeping. The mother cow was grazing seventy-five yards away. He circled down wind from her and was careful to keep out of sight, but when he turned his head aside, her sharp eyes caught sight of him before he slid again into a deep cluster of brush near the sleeping calf.

The first warning of the cow's approach came when her head and shoulders crashed through the brush, and he was almost caught upon the points of her driven horns when his snarling jaws struck. The sudden rush of the cow threw him off balance, and instead of slashing the calf's throat his fangs buried in its shoulder and ripped a gash across it. Before he could recover, the cow was back upon him with a challenging bellow, and he turned to fight for his life.

When fighting a grown animal the wolf brought his assaults from the rear. Instinct sharpened by worldly knowledge had taught him that the quickest way to a cow's throat was to weaken the driving power behind those dangerous horns. Therefore he directed his attention to the heavy muscles that controlled the action of her hind legs.

The cow whirled amid a cloud of dust and drove toward him, but he ducked low and slid under the pointed horns. Before she could turn and face him again, his body flashed around in a quick circle and he dived for her rear. His fangs sank into the lower part of her thigh and he drew first blood of the contest. The sweet taste gave him new courage and confidence, but he never forgot that it would take many such strokes for him to win, while one true stab of those horns would bring about his own finish. Twice he felt the sickening sensation of being caught in the crooks of her horns and tossed high overhead; but his resilient body recovered poise in time to save himself. With the caution and cunning of his kind he darted in and struck and darted out again.

Within a few short moments he could see the coming reward. The violent exertion of the cow's quick pivots and charges was beginning to tell. She no longer whirled with the clean and forceful movements that had marked the early part of the struggle. A weariness slowed her steps to faltering stumbles. But in spite of the tide of battle turning against her, she still faced her antagonist with a stubborn courage, and gave no indication that she would seek safety through flight.

When the wolf saw the opening at her throat, he crouched low for a spring. He was halted suddenly by a heavy shock and a quick dart of pain in his chest. Instantly there followed the boom of a gun, and the bullet which passed through him from shoulder to shoulder glanced from a rock and hummed its way into space. He knew that his deadliest of all enemies was about. The explosion of a rifle was not new to him; he had been shot at before.

He gasped for breath, but none came. A choking gurgle from the depths of his throat arose, along with a smothering nausea. His legs sagged weakly and his lips parted, exposing a double row of gleaming teeth — locked together in deadly pain. His head went up in defiance to all his foes and he tried to sound the death howl, but not even a hiss came from between those clinched teeth. Both lungs had collapsed. His body arched and heaved in his fight for breath. He folded his legs and sank to the ground and his massive head came to rest upon outstretched paws. The pupils of large yellow eyes rolled back in their sockets, and his dying vision settled upon the head and shoulders of a man.

The head and shoulders belonged to Bill Sanders. He was sitting upon his horse above the brow of a hill, two hundred yards away. The short barrel of a Winchester carbine rested across the fork of his saddle and a stray wisp of smoke oozed from its muzzle.

'Well, Old Spindleshanks,' Bill was saying to his horse. 'When Old Aunt Betsy speaks, she's real emphatic.'

When Bill arrived upon the scene, a quick change overcame him. The little tune he was whistling came no longer from pursed lips. Deep blue eyes that could twinkle in good humor reached a steady focus. A large mouth that was usually spread in a friendly grin snapped shut in hard lines. His six feet of lean body stiffened from booted heel to sombrero-covered head. Shoulders squared and narrow hips twisted in the saddle as he reached for and drew his Winchester from its scabbard. A hurried sight and quick pressure of the trigger followed. The gun roared its detonation and the wolf had staggered to its death. Old Aunt Betsy had spoken. She seldom needed to speak twice when Bill Sanders peeped through the sights and pulled the trigger.

'Good Old Aunt Betsy,' Bill murmured as he replaced the weapon and rode ahead.

'Hell!' he ejaculated, with a mixture of surprise and exultation. He dismounted and made closer inspection of the dead wolf. He noted the animal's grizzled head, the frost-scarred ears, and the three toes missing from the right front foot. 'It ain't nobody but Ol' Slaughterhouse hisself that has gone the route of all killer wolves.'

'I'll just get me a trophy, as the big-game hunter says,' Bill grinned to himself. He dropped to his knee beside the wolf and whetted the blade of his knife across his boot sole.

Before he was through with his task of skinning, he was interrupted by a sobbing bleat. He looked up and saw an old cow trying to comfort her trembling calf while she licked blood from the wound on its shoulder.

'Now, ain't that a shame!' the cowboy said. 'You pore little feller. Pore little "Sancho"!' — meaning pet. 'You and yo'r mammy both had a close call. You ain't the first little sancho calf that this old Slaughterhouse ever ripped open — but you're the last.'

Bill stood up and looked at the ugly gash. A light of admiration crept into his eyes as he regarded the mother cow, which had turned her attention from the calf to him and now stood waving her long and graceful horns in a defiant challenge.

'You've got a good mammy, little Sancho,' he said. 'She'll fight for you until you grow a pair of horns just like hers so's you can fight for yo'self.' He took a step nearer, and the cow turned away, followed by her calf.

CHAPTER TWO
THE TREE TOP OUTFIT

THE land where Sancho first saw the light of day was the home range of the Tree Top Ranch, which embraced five hundred square miles of virgin grass land. Natural lines formed the boundaries. It lay for a distance of twenty-five miles along the Colorado River front on the north, while twenty miles to the south, it was hedged in by a range of rough, brush-covered hills known as the Brady Mountains. Five principal creeks with their sources in the mountain chain cut the range at intervals of a few miles and ended at the river on the north.

To this empire of unfenced land and the thousands of cattle inhabiting it, belonged the calf which Bill Sanders had, in a mood of sympathy, called Sancho. Laws of the land and customs of the country defined ownership of a calf by the brand its mother wore. Standing out upon the mother cow's left side in distinct and graceful lines was ♈, known over the cattle country as the Tree Top brand.

The outfit was owned by Robert H. ('Old Hoss') Denman, a man of sixty-five years, with a close-clipped iron-gray mustache. He was dignified in bearing, honorable in his dealings, and dependable to the last degree. His resourcefulness had won him the title of the 'Old Wheel Horse' among his friends. His own men had taken a short cut at the title and referred to him simply as the 'Old Hoss.'

Numbered among his men was the twenty-five-year-old Bill Sanders, who ranked in authority second only to the high boss, christened Jonathan Bannister Jones but who was known simply as Banjy. Standing beside Bill's giant young framework Banjy appeared squat and middle-aged. His piercing black eyes harmonized with his dark mustache, blended with a sprinkling of gray hairs which showed his fifty years of age. His long body supported a pair of heavy stooped shoulders, and years in the saddle had curved his stumpy legs to fit the sides of a horse. A green-tipped feather of a duck's wing was always to be found sticking in his hatband.

The Old Hoss was a good judge of men, and his outfit was hand-picked to fit his needs. Bill Sanders had come to him a spindling boy of seventeen, and he had developed into a resourceful man. His loyalty and keen perception of the cattle business in all its stages had won him a place in the hearts of both the Old Hoss and Banjy. Bill did not know that they were shaping him to take high command of the outfit when Banjy's age forced him to step down and out.

Others of the clan were Dave Houston, high-strung and combative, and famed for his science with the lariat. There was Bob Long, who enjoyed an enviable reputation as an expert bronco buster; Bud West, known as a happy-go-lucky type of an all-round cowhand who took life with a jest and was ready to gamble with either money or fate. There was old Meletone, the grizzled Mexican horse-wrangler who was responsible for the Spanish flavor of the outfit's speech. *Sancho* was his word for a pet, and *remuda* applied to a bunch of saddle horses. Last but not least by any means was the Negro cook, known simply as 'Nig,' who held sway in ranch kitchen and around the chuck wagon. Added to these were nearly a score of others, including line riders, common cowhands, and teamsters, each fitting well into place in the operation of the cow outfit.

Now, with the coming of April, a tinctured aroma of spring filled the air. Soft buds no longer able to stay housed against the seductive sunshine were bursting into tender leaf clusters upon tree and bush. Spindling shoots of new grass were forcing themselves through the weather-faded mat of the old, blending the turf into a greenish brown. Cattle had lost appetite for the dry grass of last year and were shifting about in a wild scramble for the limited supply of new feed. There was also another reason for restlessness among them. Unnatural forces had been set in motion all over the range land — the general spring roundup-was in full swing.

Banjy led the Tree Top outfit onto the range and set it to work in the task of gathering the year's crop of two-year-old steers. They had been out for two weeks, and with a clatter and rattle and bang the riders were sweeping over the domain like a prairie fire. They pulled into camp below the headquarters ranch on the lower Mustang Creek and prepared for the last and hardest day's work of the season. Nig had been instructed to have an early breakfast, and the dark hour before dawn found the men silent and sleepy, following Banjy from camp, awaiting his orders that would separate them and send them upon the long circle around the high rim which marked the Mustang's watershed.

As darkness wore away and the eerie voices of night-prowling animals were stilled by the chirp and hum of day noises, Sancho stood watching his mother clip the scattering sprigs of new grass. The faint yell of a cowboy brought his head around to attention. He had never heard a sound of this kind, and he cocked his ears. Several minutes of listening brought scattered repetitions of the strange noises, which were growing nearer and louder.

His eyes swept the distant hills across the canyon above, and he discovered straggling lines of objects winding their way from the high ground toward the valley. Wherever he looked he saw other objects, moving in the same direction, that proved to be lines of running cattle.

Bill Sanders came into sight over the bulge of a knoll and galloped along the ridge above, turning all cattle toward the low ground. Close behind him rode Dave Houston, who, with loud yells and the pops of his quirt tail against chap legs, shooed them along at a faster gait. A bunch of animals grazing higher up the draw swept past Sancho and his mother. She raised her head and, calling impatiently for him to follow, she trotted into line.

Like the roll of flood waters, cattle were now pouring from all side draws and canyons. Now and then a cowboy sent a new bunch scrambling across sloping sags and steep hillsides into the creek bottom. Racing, scampering calves; rollicking, bawling steers and heifers; slow-moving, ill tempered bulls; sedate, maternal cows — all these figured in the immense gathering which riders on sweat-soaked horses moved toward the round-up ground.

The confusion increased as the large herd was pressed closer together. Strange bulls — each a monarch in his own domain — bellowed loud challenges and engaged in deadly combat. Two of them clashed near Sancho, and they surged back and forth with the tide of battle, their huge bulks sweeping aside any obstruction in their line of maneuvers.

Thus it was that when Sancho followed his mother into that vast gathering, there were so many new things happening that he forgot all about her. After being jostled around by other roving animals and knocked flat by one of them fleeing before the charge of a fighting bull, he sought her for comfort, but she was not to be found. He bawled for her, but his call was drowned by the sound of a thousand other lost calves.

Bill Sanders and Banjy paused and turned their horses to look over another bunch scattered along a side hill which flanked the round-up ground. They were all steer cattle, grazing quietly while four men rode back and forth holding them in a loose formation. These steers had been gathered in the two weeks before, and with the five hundred in this round-up the herd would number two thousand head, to be started immediately upon a long journey to faraway Kansas.

Spread out over a small level bench of a foothill, between the day herd of steers and the round-up of milling cattle, was the camp outfit. In the center of a scattered litter of beds, corral ropes, and other camp equipment was the chuck wagon. A tall box with a sloping front protruded from the rear end of the wagon bed and stood wide open, displaying neat rows of loaded shelves within. The let-down lid of the box was serving as a kitchen table, and stood propped up by a hinged leg.

Dividing his time between the campfire and table, Nig was hurriedly and skillfully preparing a meal for more than twenty ravenous appetites. Rounding away from the opposite side of the wagon into a huge oval was the tightly stretched rope corral. Old Meletone was pushing the *remuda* of saddle horses toward the wide-open gap, singing one of his Spanish songs not at all complimentary to the hard-riding men who wore away horseflesh upon the long circles of the round-up.

Riding into camp in small groups, the men dismounted and each roped the horse of his choice, hurriedly saddled him and made a wild dash back to the round-up.

Banjy and Bill Sanders held another brief consultation, which resulted in fifteen men scattering around the main bunch of cattle in position to hold them in place. Bill, Banjy, and Dave Houston, now mounted upon their favorite cutting horses, rode into the round-up and started cutting out the two-year-old steers.

The contests which developed when the skill of the trained cow pony was pitted against the crafty and impulsive tricks of the daring steers furnished a new and interesting entertainment for Sancho. He stood watching the quick-footed horses lunge forward in short spurts, then whirl around and turn low amid the clouds of dust as they checkmated obstinate steers in their bids for liberty; and there was born in Sancho's mind a longing to try his own speed and cunning against the horse.

In time Sancho's interest was claimed by hunger. He was bumped and knocked hither and there as he worked his way around through the milling cattle in a vain hunt for his mother. After a long search, he decided that in some manner she had made her escape, and guided by his calf instinct he edged his way around to the back side of the herd and sneaked out. He started away slowly, bawling as he went, but he had covered only a short distance when one of the herders galloped around and turned him back. Next time he started off in a half gallop and half run, but he found that the horse could run much faster and he was soon outdistanced. Pain was added to his humiliation when the herder unloosed several coils of his rope and whipped him back among the cattle.

When the work was halted for the noon meal, there was little or no rest for Sancho and his mourning calf-mates. The charging horses no longer stirred them around, but an uneasiness continued as frantic mothers trotted here and there hunting their lost babies and hungry calves bawled hoarsely.

The work dragged painfully into mid-afternoon. The blazing sun beat down with a steady fire. Not a breath of wind arose to drift away the heavy clouds of dust, cut into a fine powder and stirred up by thousands of shuffling feet. The sleek and frisky horses which had been ridden away from the corral such a short time ago, now sweat-drenched and dust-covered, were panting for breath, while weary men with parched lips and sunburned faces urged them on, and hungry cattle jostled and hooked each other around in their miserable confusion.

As the number of two-year-old steers became scarcer and the men were forced to hunt longer for them, the work gradually slowed up. The cattle calmed down, and many cows and their calves were being happily reunited. Sancho's hope of finding his mother revived, and now he was so absorbed in his search for her that he failed to note the happenings around him. When he discovered that there was a change, he found that he was free.

The bunch of cattle in which he had been held so closely were scattering in all directions. The newly gathered steers had been taken over by the day herders, and were being mixed with the other and quieter animals. Dust-covered men were unsaddling tired horses at the camp; Old Meletone was again driving his *remuda* back toward the rope corral, looking with disapproval at the exhausted horses so recently turned loose. Other men were catching night horses, and Nig was busy spreading out a heartening supper for all hands.

Sancho was again bewildered at the new confusion of bawling cattle scattering from the round-up and starting back to their native range. Then his natural instinct took hold of his mind and guided his footsteps. He struck out confidently toward the place where he had last seen his mother.

He found her, and after feeding to the full capacity of his stomach, he stretched out on the ground to rest. He dozed away into restless slumber amid a series of bad dreams. He kicked and bawled in his sleep, but when morning came he faced an entirely different world from the one of the day before. The dazzling sunlight and peaceful stillness drove away all his fears and troubled thoughts. He did not know that the round-up was over, and that the herd of steers were now being shaped upon the first leg of their long trip over the Kansas trail, where all tracks led out and none led back.

While Banjy was whipping his trail outfit into shape for the long drive, every cowhand in the country was decking out in his gladdest rags or already riding toward the Tree Top headquarters, counting the hours and miles that intervened between them and the one gala event of the year — the dance and supper in celebration of the departure of the trail herd. From Coleman Town fifty miles away and from every ranch and hamlet within a radius of a like distance they came. They came in carriages, buggies, and wagons and on horseback, and with her relatives from Coleman Town came Virginia Lowe.

As self-appointed welcomers, Bud West and Bob Long met each contingent of arriving guests and entertained them with daring feats of horsemanship. With her blue eyes shining in wonder at the strange surroundings, Virginia passed into the house. From where he was standing on the front porch Bill Sanders had his first glimpse of the new girl, and he forgot the discomfort of being dressed up in his best suit of clothes and a pair of patent-leather shoes that seemed hellbent on crushing the life out of his feet, and the stiff white collar that gouged unmercifully in the region of his tonsils.

The large dining-room had been cleared of all furniture except a row of chairs around the wall. At one end of the room was a temporary rostrum where sat Banjy and old Meletone. The strings of Banjy's fiddle whined in protest as he plunked them sharply in seeking his proper chord. With the base of his Mexican harp resting against his left shoulder, old Meletone ran his delicate fingers over the maze of strings in loving caress. Then the dance started. 'Grab yo'r partners, fellers, and hit the timber with yo'r leather,' called Dave Houston in the rôle of floor manager. The strains of 'Over the Waves' filled the room, and Bill saw Virginia offer her arm to her uncle as the floor filled with gliding couples.

Bill watched, a little envious, as one cowboy after another claimed her for a dance, and he regretted that his shyness had prevented him from mastering the intricate steps of the quadrille and schottische. When he finally managed to get an introduction to her, she surprised him by asking point-blank with a mischievous twinkle in her eyes if he would dance the next set with her.

'I just cain't cut the mustard,' Bill confessed. 'But I'd like mighty well to set one out with you,' he blurted; and then he wondered what he had said.

'Life is too gay and the night too short to waste time sitting with a clumsy-wumsy that can't dance,' Virginia laughed, and danced away from him into a group of admiring cowboys.

The ripple of laughter that ran around the hall reminded Bill that his awkwardness had again got him into trouble. With his face a blistering red, he sidled from the room and met Bud West in the doorway.

'I saw that play,' Bud said, 'and I'm about half sore. You need a little sniffer to steady yo'rself,' he continued, producing a whiskey flask from his pocket.

'But the Old Hoss——' Bill started to protest.

'Yeah, I know he'd raise hell and put a chunk under it if he found out, but what he don't know won't hurt nobody,' Bud hastened to say.

Still burning from embarrassment and under the genial influence of Bud West, Bill took hair-scorching swallows from the bottle and cast aside the guilty knowledge that he was violating the strictest injunction of the Old Hoss by drinking on dance night.

'I'll git a dance with her and give 'er all she wants of it,' Bud boasted. 'I'll swing 'er so hard her toes'll pop like a whipcracker.' And saying this he pushed his way onto the dance floor.

True to his word, Bud started out to give Virginia a wild demonstration of a wild man's dance. Bill saw a look of consternation appear upon her face, and he was about to interfere when Dave Houston clapped Bud roughly upon the shoulder and stopped the couple. Bill flashed a quick glance at Banjy, who was watching everything. Without moving the base of his fiddle from its place under his chin and without hesitating in the stroke of his bow, Banjy caught Bill's eye and made ever the slightest jerk with his head. Bill knew what the gesture meant. He knew that Banjy was reminding him that no love or friendship existed between the hot-headed Dave Houston and the reckless Bud West. Banjy was ordering him to interfere and prevent a fight upon the dance floor.

Virginia stood a little to one side with a mixed expression of excitement and alarm. It was plain that she had never been in a situation of this kind, and she was uncertain as to what she should do. Bill could see the anger mounting on the drink-flushed face of Bud West, and he could see a twitching in the doubled fists of Dave Houston. Bill walked over and laid his hand upon Dave's arm.

'I'll take care of this,' he said, moving between the belligerents.

'I'm sorry this happened, Miss,' he continued, stepping close to Virginia, forgetting the smell of liquor on his own breath. 'Bud's all right, but he's just drinkin' a little, which none of us approve of on dance night.'

Virginia backed away with a genuine look of anger on her face. 'You must be drunk yourself,' she said, with her eyes sparkling defiance.

Bill led Bud out of the house burning with anger. He was mad at Bud, mad at Dave, and mad at the girl. He threw Bud roughly upon a bed in the bunkhouse. He started out the door and then turned squarely around and re-entered. He tore the white collar from his neck and threw it out the window. He removed his tight-fitting shoes and slung them in different directions. He pulled on his boots and walked outside. He mounted his horse and rode out to the herd, where four men were waiting impatiently for the end of their guard period. There Bill stayed until the dust had settled from the last departing guest and he knew that the dance was over. Daylight found him still smarting from the snub of the night before. After helping Banjy start the herd away, he retired to the bunkhouse to ease his wounded feelings in slumber.

CHAPTER THREE
SANCHO LOSES
A HORN

B ILL met the responsibility of managing the ranch during Banjy's absence in his own methodical way. He installed the usual line riders in the various camps, where they endeavored to keep the Tree Top cattle from straying from the range. While scouting back and forth between his line camps and headquarters, observing all cattle in general, he failed to notice one particular long-horned cow and her rapidly developing calf, but many times from the mirage of sun-bleached plain, he did see the face of a girl as she accused him of being drunk.

Sancho's growth was rapid, and it appeared that he would exceed his mother in size. His lengthy stride and easy movement showed great speed and unknown limits of travel in those long legs. The sharp pegs sprouting from the side of his head promised to grow into horns with a spread of at least four feet. In color he bore a striking resemblance to his Hereford sire, with a cherry-red body and white face and breast.

As the season drew into fall, Sancho felt a change. The grass was curing into a firm texture; the nights were getting cooler and cooler and his hair was fuzzing out into a heavier coat. The sun's brilliance was dimming, and thousands of migrating fowl were flying high overhead in odd-shaped formations on their way to wintering grounds in the southern marshes.

And while Sancho and his mother with many other cattle were grazing higher and higher among the Brady Mountain foothills, the Tree Top cowboys were preparing for the final task of the season.

Banjy and his trail men with their remuda of travel-worn saddle horses returned from the north. Bill Sanders and the ranch hands were anxiously awaiting them with fresh mounts and ready branding irons.

Thus it was upon a morning in September that Sancho was again disturbed by the presence of men on horseback as they charged over the country and swung their ropes and raised the dust of another round-up. The number in this gathering was much smaller than the one before. Now the calves had little trouble in keeping up with their mothers. As for Sancho, he had grown indifferent except at feeding time, and it mattered little to him where he was. Along with this indifference, he had developed an insubordination toward any kind of authority, and he strutted brazenly into the round-up.

Each cow with her calf following alongside was cut from the round-up and moved to a separate bunch. When all the calves had been cut out, the main bunch of cattle were shunted to one side and turned loose. The cows and calves were then driven to a spot where two men were dragging up wood with ropes fastened to their saddle horns. A third was sticking branding irons into a blazing fire.

'Fall into yo'r places, fellers,' called Banjy as he pulled an iron from the fire and noted its temperature.

Then turning around he scanned the faces about him and his gaze came to rest upon Bill Sanders. 'You goin' to do the markin' and trimmin', Bill? — and see that the boys git the brands on straight?' At Bill's nod, Banjy continued with his orders.

'Bob, you handle the irons and keep the fire punched up. Dave, you do the twinin' and four of you hit the ground and do the flankin'. Bud, you and the rest of the grub-wasters scatter out and hold that bunch of cows and calves together durin' this ceremony.'

While Sancho watched the men go to their appointed places, Dave Houston rode into the little bunch, uncoiling a rope and shaking it into a loop. He flipped the loop over the head of a calf which was standing unsuspectingly at Sancho's side. The calf stood in bewildered fear, then whirled into wild flight; the trained horse turned toward the branding fire and the rope dragged the struggling calf to its painful experience. One of the footmen walked out, and with an easy motion grabbed one ear and a flank and crashed it to the ground. Sancho at once sensed impending danger, and forgetting his bravado buried himself deeply among the other cattle. Within a short time both sets of flankers were on the ground holding down calves, while Bob Long hurried back and forth with hot branding irons and Bill Sanders plied his knife.

Sancho watched his mother during these times and tried to take courage from her complacent attitude. He remembered that a man was around every time he suffered physical pain. There was an ominous threat in the atmosphere of those grim-faced men, and there was carried to him a premonition of disaster in the whirr of that loop as Dave Houston cast it with deadly skill around the necks of frightened calves.

Calf after calf was dragged to the branding fire; bawls of fright and pain came to Sancho, and he sniffed warily at the scent of burning hair and scorching flesh which drifted to him as the red-hot iron seared the Tree Top brand. He maintained a close watch upon the roper, and contrived to keep many cattle between himself and the threat of danger by gliding quickly and silently around like a restless panther.

Three times Dave flung his widespread and spinning loop at his head and missed. In each instance the throw was long, and Sancho extremely quick. These miscasts had not gone unnoticed by the cowboys, who appeared to derive joyful satisfaction and voiced their feelings in chiding comment.

'What you ropin' at, Dave?' sang out a voice as the loop spread itself around a cluster of brush over which Sancho's head had been an instant before.

'He's jus' practicin' up on somethin' that cain't move,' rejoined another.

'Why don't you sprinkle a little salt on his tail?' called out Bud West. 'When I was a boy and tried to ketch birds and such like, my Pap always told me that a little salt sprinkled in the right place would make 'em gentle.'

Dave flipped the honda of his rope into his hand and ran it into another loop. A red flush crept under the tan of his skin, and he bit into his lower lip and replied to the taunts.

'Keep still, little children. Keep still. You're liable to rattle yo'r mental'ty loose. You poochers jus' take it easy and don't overjump yo'rselves. Jus' tend to yo'r herdin' and don't try to help me with the rope-flingin'. It'll be lots easier on you.'

At last, when Sancho was the only unbranded calf remaining, he caught Dave Houston's eye fixed upon him and instinct told him that his time had come. That is, it had almost come. He knew with the same instinct that his newly learned trick of gliding behind other cattle would not work for him now, but he remembered that another chance of escape was open, and he felt a strong urge to take it.

It was true, he remembered, that his other attempt to outrun a horse had turned out a painful failure, but he had no fear of failure now — not if he could get past that line of men. Recent trials at play had led him to believe that he could outrun anything that walked upon four legs.

Less than two hundred yards away, a thick mott of brush beckoned to all his daring impulse. Brush was the place for a calf that was seeking shelter.

While circling around to a point nearest the brush clump, he saw Dave Houston riding through the cattle and coming straight toward him. He knew that a few more strides of the horse would bring the deadly loop within reach, and he turned to brave the danger of the riders outside.

The horsemen whom he feared seemed to care little or nothing about him. On the contrary, his sudden flight brought loud cheers of encouragement from all bystanders.

'Jus' look at 'im! Jus' look at 'im run! He's got his ears laid back and movin' like a streak of lightnin'.'

'Go to it, little feller. Go to it! I hope you make yo'r getaway,' shouted Bud West. 'I'm for you stronger'n hossradish!'

Bud whirled his horse around until he was facing Dave Houston. 'Who wants to bet money that he don't make the brush?'

Dave Houston was working his way out of the herd as fast as he could without running over the tightly packed cattle. He had reached the outer edge and raised his rope aloft ready to whip his horse into a run. He turned and looked at Bud.

'I'll take five dollars' worth of that money,' retorted Dave. He slashed his horse low on the thigh and the animal lunged ahead into a run.

'Make it ten!' yelled Bud shrilly; but his words were wasted. The roar of the wind rushing past Dave's head drowned out all sound.

Sancho was fifty yards in the lead before the horse leveled off into his running stride, but now the gap was closing up between them. The fleeing calf looked back and saw the horse, stretched out low, his nose thrust forward, leaping in gigantic strides while the loop of that whistling rope swung with rhythmic precision. Sancho could hear dimly the shouts and laughter of the cowboys around the branding fire. He looked ahead at the clump of sheltering brush. A few more leaps would put him behind its screen of protecting limbs where no rope could reach him. From the corner of his eye he saw another rider, who appeared to have entered the chase. Bud West was speeding alongside to witness the outcome of the race and his wager, but he kept a safe distance away.

The rattle of loose stones and pounding hoofbeats caused Sancho to look backward and he became terror-stricken. That roping-horse was now almost upon him. Dave Houston stood balanced in his stirrups — leaning slightly forward — poised to make his throw.

Sancho gathered all his strength and put it into one great leap for safety. Then he heard the whish and whirr of a rope cut the air as the fast-sailing loop spun and gyrated above his head. Something wispy and strange pulled around his neck.

The trained horse stopped with one rough plunge and braced himself for the impact that experience had taught him would follow. The rope had tightened around Sancho's neck when he made his wild leap for cover, and he was caught off balance. He took up the slack and dropped heavily amid a bed of rocks with his neck doubled under. There was a sharp crack of broken bone, and when he struggled to his feet, his left horn was dangling from its shattered base. A thin stream of blood trickled over his eye and marked a red streak across the white of his jaw.

'How do you poochers like that?' called out Dave Houston. He whirled his horse and started towing the breathless calf toward the branding fire. 'He's a little bunged up, but he's on the end of my twine jus' the same. If there's any more of you long-haired dodgers that's got five dollars to lose, I'll turn 'im loose and do it all over agin. It's jus' like takin' candy away from a baby,' he finished.

'You ort to have had it understood that the goods was to be delivered undamaged, Bud,' laughed Bill Sanders.

'Never mind that part,' retorted Bud. 'If he's game, I'll get that five back with heavy interest before night.'

In spite of the noose cutting off his breath, Sancho dug his toes into the ground and fought his best. When they neared the fire, one of the flankers walked out to meet them and seized the rope near his head. He made another wild leap and was again caught off balance. This time he crashed to the ground broadside, with the two flankers landing in his middle.

The pain of his broken horn was blinding, but this faded away when the hot branding iron seered into his flesh and traced a charred mark over his body. He made futile and desperate struggles against the strength of two flankers as Bob Long burned the line of the Tree Top brand into his left side.

'That's the last one, boys,' said Banjy, mounting his horse. 'They're all branded now, and you can turn the herd loose.'

Banjy started drifting the cattle away. He galloped around the lead and turned them up a slight hill, leaving the rear unattended, and Sancho's mother turned back toward the branding fire.

She stamped the ground and bellowed a low warning. Then she lowered her head and charged.

'Look out there, fellers — there she comes!' warned Bud West. She made a determined charge at Bob Long and overtook him halfway between Sancho and the branding fire. This sudden outburst of a fighting mood brought another chorus of cheers from the group of men, who appeared quick to show their admiration of a fighting spirit.

'Climb a tree!' — 'Jump over the moon!' — 'Crawl in a hole and pull the hole in after you!' were some of the gibes thrown at the threatened man, who dodged back and forth, warding off the cow's attack with a branding iron.

'I'll bet five dollars that she hooks a hole in the seat of his pants yet,' bantered Bud West. Then Bill Sanders swung into his saddle and moved to rescue the threatened cowboy by driving his horse against the cow's side.

'What do you fellers mean?' he demanded angrily. 'You stand there laughin' like a pack of fools while a man is about to get a cow's horn drove through his body.' The impact of Bill's horse pushed her around, and he drove on until she was outside the circle of men.

'Now hold that cow out there until this calf is branded and turned loose,' Bill ordered, with a glare at the men around him, whose mirth was stilled. 'You fellers're goin' to get a man killed some of these days while yo're playin' hoss like a bunch of kids. It's a good thing Banjy didn't see this sideshow; he'd fire the whole damned bunch,' he finished.

What a hell cat!' sighed Bob Long as he leaned against his own horse and panted for breath. 'No wonder that calf is such a wild little devil with a mammy like her. I bet she'd lick the teeth out of a buzz saw.'

Bill Sanders dismounted and finished his own task with the calf. He paused above it with open knife. He looked at the mother and whistled softly. He leaned over Sancho and brushed the hair upon his shoulder and exposed to view the tracings of a dim scar. Then Bill smiled.

'I'll be skinned alive if it ain't my little Sancho pet,' he mumbled. 'You've done got into trouble again, ain't you, little feller?'

Bill looked down at the broken horn, and then performed the only act of mercy for the day when he leaned over and severed the shreds of hide which held the mangled bone and horn together.

'Pore little Sancho,' he said soothingly. 'You ain't got but one horn to fight yo'r battles with now, and you'll have to be sort of careful about the fights you match.'

When Sancho was released from the holds of the flankers, he staggered to his feet in a bewildered daze. His mother rushed forward with disregard to the cowboys, and tried to soothe him by licking the brand and his bleeding head. But nothing could ease his pain and wounded spirit now. When he retreated with his mother into the solitude of the range, he was burning with hate for the men who were so deft with their ropes and so cruel with their knives and branding irons.

Within a month the strips of hide which marked the lines of his brand had peeled off and the wound healed over, leaving a permanent scar. There was a thin layer of tender hide edging its way over the round hole in the side of his head where the horn had been torn away.

As time assuaged his mental anguish and nature cured his physical wounds, he would have viewed life in a lighter vein, had not another disturbing element forged its way into his being.

The days of Indian summer were giving way before the onslaughts of winter, and Sancho was conscious of a change in his mother. Flesh was shrinking from her frame, exposing sharp back and hip bones. Her milk supply had dwindled and she had grown indifferent toward him. Of late, his attempts at suckling had met with painful rebuffs. Sharp rakes of horns across his rump or stinging blows against his head from her hoofs were the answer when he tried to draw the small supply of milk from her collapsed udder. He did not know that she was going through the natural process of rebuilding her strength in order to bring another calf into the world and bestow upon it the same nourishing care she had given him.

After Sancho's weaning, the ties of parenthood were so strong that he stayed with his mother all winter, but when the first sprigs of grass appeared with returning spring, the ties became looser and he finally put the old cow out of his mind forever and drifted out over the range upon his own.

A year of Sancho's life went by with little incident to mark the passage of time. He roamed the Tree Top range, and developed in both size and worldly wisdom. When caught in roundups, the painful experience of other occasions was recalled and he employed all his tricks of evasion with wild and spectacular dashes for freedom.

Thus he grew into a full-fledged two-year-old steer; tall and lank of body, quick and active in motion, wild by nature, and wary at any hint of danger.

CHAPTER FOUR

ON THE TRAIL

T HE prophecy of seasonal harbingers had been fulfilled. All plant life broke out in a resplendent coat of green. Cattle were shedding tangled mats of dead hair and showing their response to the stimulating effects of green grass. The call of mating plover rolled across hill and prairie and blended with the resonant voice of bullfrogs along the watercourses.

With his hat feather cocked at a jaunty angle and the rowels of his spurs jingling to the motion of his horse, Banjy swung the Tree Top outfit into action. Two weeks of hard circle riding and slashing round-up work had netted a residue of two thousand steers. Into this sea of restless animals had fallen Sancho, and much against his will he was being drifted with the herd to the northern border of the range. Upon the morning of April 15, he walked from the bed ground after spending his first night under guard.

A south wind whipped low-sailing Gulf clouds across a dull sky. Huge bullbats with their ominous calls swooped low and suddenly wheeled aloft. Streaks of early morning sunlight sifted through flying clouds and slitted over the tops of green foliage. As the herd edged toward the rough breaks flanking the Colorado River, Sancho pushed his way to the front and tilted his nose aloft, seeking to fathom the source of the odd smell of muddy water. He paused upon the high bluff overlooking the river valley and viewed the twisting stream for the first time in his life, and sniffed wisely. With his curiosity fully aroused, he plunged down the steep hillside and led out across the bottom land. But when he saw the muddy water churning itself into a red foam, pouring over boulders and ledges of a rough shoal, he whirled back in alarm.

From his station on the right point, Bud West noted Sancho's alarm and laughed out loud.

'Look at Old Long Legs,' he called to Bob Long. 'He took one look at the river and turned back so quick that he nearly popped his tail off. He don't think water was made for anything but to drink. He's sort of shy about touchin' it with anything but his mouth. He never heard about water bein' good to take a bath in. He's sort of like some cowpunchers.'

'Yeah,' replied Bob. 'Before we hit the high plains of Kansas he'll git lots of baths. And that's where he's sort of like some cow-punchers I know too. He's got a lot to learn.'

Sancho bored his way to the rear of the herd and was turned back by a drag driver. Everywhere he looked was a man on horse-back blocking his escape, and he reluctantly drifted along with the string of walking cattle to the river bank. Cattle were now pouring across the stream in closely packed columns and were spreading over the north bank and sinking into the brush. This apparent outlet to safety pulled strong against his fear of the water. When the current whipped along his sides, he was seized with a wild panic and once more whirled and leaped for safety on dry ground.

'Git along there, little dogy,' laughed Bill Sanders, tossing the loose coils of his rope along Sancho's back. 'You ain't so water-shy as you make out. Wait till you git soused in some real water.'

Bill Sanders and Banjy were riding side by side discussing ranch affairs, and they paused on the river bank to watch the cattle wade into the water.

As the coils of Bill's rope draped across his back, Sancho was again gripped with fear. With a loud snort and with his back arched into a steep hump, he sprang high into the air and dived off the bank into the water half-side deep. He went stone blind at the muddy water splashing into his wide-open eyes, but he did not wait to get his bearings. He plunged madly ahead, depending upon instinctive reckoning for a guide. He stumbled over loose rock and rolling boulders in his frenzy, and before he realized it the water was receding from his body and he came out upon a dry gravel-bar on the far side. He lost no time in scrambling up the bank and losing himself in the fringe of brush.

'Take good care of my little pet steer,' admonished Bill.

'I'll take good care to land 'im in Kansas,' replied Banjy drily. 'From the way he's friskin' around he's goin' to need takin' care of.'

'He'll be all right when he gets used to things,' Bill condoned. 'He's jus' nervous and scared now. He'll settle down to business in a day or two.'

'Yeah,' replied Banjy wisely. 'But he's liable to raise a lot of hell and stir things up before he decides to settle down. I always aim to spot them nervous ones first and watch 'em a little closer than the common run — and this feller is already on my list. But we'll git 'im there all right,' he finished confidently, turning in his saddle and looking back.

Banjy at once busied himself with the problem of starting the herd upon the trail. He directed Nig with the wagon, and Meletone with his hundred and more head of saddle horses, to the night camp spot. Other crisp orders sent his crew of nine cowboys to their designated stations around the herd. Under the combined pressure of his own and Bill's crew, the herd formed into a trailing line and wound its way from the brushy river bottom out onto the open hills.

Bill Sanders and his men gathered in a small group on the first hill and watched the herd move away. His eyes scanned the walking animals until his gaze rested upon Sancho. 'Good-bye, little feller,' said Bill. 'You'll grow big and fat and make good beef for somebody,' he finished as he turned and rode away.

Sancho at once set out on a tour of investigation. He wormed and hooked his way from one end of the line to the other, and three miles were covered before he realized that he was treading upon strange ground. He edged out of the string of walking cattle and looked wistfully at the rim of green-covered hills marking the boundary of his homeland. He bawled sadly and started back toward the river, and his course of travel brought him squarely in front of Banjy, who was also upon a tour of inspection.

'No, you don't,' countered the trail boss as his horse swept quickly around the straying steer and turned him back. 'You might be a wild and woolly steer and Bill Sanders's pet to boot, but you ain't nobody else's pet by a long shot, and I don't give a hoot how wild you are. Me and these waddies 've got the medicine for all wild steers right here,' he finished, fumbling at the coiled rope on his saddle. 'You've done et yo'r last bite of Tree Top grass and guzzled yo'r last drop of Mustang Water. You're on yo'r way up the Kansas trail to make first-class beefsteak some time.'

After Banjy turned him back, Sancho forged toward the lead cattle and Banjy kept pace with him.

'Keep yo're eye peeled for that one-horned steer,' Banjy cautioned Dave Houston, who was driving the left point. 'He's snaky as a rabbit and slick as an eel, and he's liable to give us the slip any time. I'd hate to lose any steer — and much more that one. I can hear Bill Sanders givin' us that wise hoss laugh of his'n right now.

'Keep 'em movin',' was Banjy's order to his men. 'The more miles we cover before dark, the sounder they'll lay on the bed ground tonight. We'll not even stop for dinner. We'll relieve each other and keep those dogies pointed up the trail.'

Two hours before sundown, the cattle were thrown off the trail to graze and fill up before night. For the first time in the long day the men relaxed and gathered in a knot at the rear of the cattle, which were now spreading out in a fan shape ahead, hungrily devouring the plentiful grass.

'Dave,' Banjy ordered, 'you pick out a couple of waddies to stand first guard with you and then git into camp for a little rest. Bud and a couple of others can take second guard, and you other three can stand the last shift. That'll make three guards of three men each — not countin' me and old Meletone. Meletone will have his hands full lookin' after the remuda, and I'll have mine full lookin' after all of you waddies.'

'Shore,' interrupted Bud. 'I savvy all that. The first feller that's caught asleep on guard 'll git fired, and you're liable to pop up at the herd most any time of night. I've got so used to hearin' that old night hoss of yourn comin' through the dark that I can tell the fall of one foot from the other.'

'All right,' interpolated Banjy. 'Since you know all about that, you and yo'r second guard compañeros shuffle off to the wagon, and when old Meletone brings in the remuda catch up night hosses for everybody. Me and these other fellers'll keep 'em drifting along till we get 'em on the bed ground,' Banjy finished, with a sweeping wave of his hand at the grazing cattle.

Sancho was tired for the first time in his life. He was hungry too, and he made the best of his opportunity to satisfy his hunger. He and his mates grazed slowly toward the camp and were the subject of a discussion among the cowboys, which eventually wound up in a heated argument between Dave Houston and Bud West.

'What'll they do tonight, Meletone?' asked Dave, dropping his empty plate into the dishpan and seating himself for an after-supper cup of coffee and a cigarette. 'Will they be sort of peaceful-like, or will they give us entertainment durin' the guard hours?'

Old Meletone clasped both hands around his coffee cup and blew cooling breaths over the hot liquid, slanting his eyes at the setting sun. 'Mebbe so, mebbe no,' he replied slowly. 'The sun she luke like wind blow tonight theesaway. When wind blow——'

'I ain't afraid of no run,' interrupted Bud. 'They've had their dew claws run off of 'em all day long and cattle've got a little sense. They'll rest when they get a chance——'

'Who wants yo'r opinion?' asked Dave, fixing Bud with a scornful stare.

'You wanted to know, didn't you?' rasped Bud. 'You needn't git on the peck so sudden. I just answered yo'r question.'

'I ain't askin' you nothin',' retorted Dave. 'Meletone has done forgot more'n you'll ever learn if you live a hundred years. You might know how to jockey a hoss race or slip a cold deck of cards into a poker game — but when that's said and done you're plumb out——'

'I back my words with money — which is more'n you've got nerve to do,' Bud slapped his pocket.

A slow smile lit up Dave's face. He pulled a fat wallet from the hip pocket and laid it upon his knee. 'Here's a hundred dollars. I'll bet any of it, from ten up, that the herd runs tonight,' he said solemnly.

Bud reached for his own pocket and then stopped.

'I've fell into my own trap,' he said. 'Wouldn't I be a real sucker to make a bet like that?' he asked. 'All you'd have to do would be to rattle a slicker or strike a match sometime durin' yo'r guard, and then — whff! away they'd go.'

'All right, then,' Dave retorted. 'Keep yo'r lip buttoned up when gents are talkin'!'

Old Meletone listened to the rough bantering with polite indifference. When it was finished, he resumed where he left off. 'The waither she luke like blow tonight. Wind she make cattle too nairvous — some time she go meel roun' and roun' an' then run like hell. Mebbe so she go run tonight.'

Dave Houston dumped the grounds from his coffee cup and slung it in the general direction of the dishpan. He hitched up the belt to his chaps and strode to his night horse. He gathered up his bridle reins and stood poised with one foot in the stirrup and the other on the ground.

'Thanks, Meletone. You've bore me out in my own deductions and helped me make a wise guy shut his mouth. You don't offer much consolation to a little boy that's scared of the dark and runnin' cattle, but thanks just the same,' he finished. He swung his leg over the horse's back and led his two night herders out to where Banjy was rounding the herd into a compact mass upon the bed ground.

Sancho was far from satisfied with his present surroundings. There were too many cattle close to him and there were too many men around. He liked fresh, clean grass to lie upon, and before a single animal lay down to rest the bed ground was cut into a soft mulch.

In spite of all this he lay down to rest. His sleep became fitful. He lay choking and gasping for breath, and a shiver ran over his stiffened body. Consciousness returned through his sense of hearing when a low rumbling arose around him. When he broke the unseen bonds holding him so still, he bounded to his feet and was caught in a surge of running animals. The phantom of his dreams was nowhere in evidence, but a swarm of frenzied cattle plunged away into the darkness.

Like any good trail man, Banjy slept with one eye open. On picket near his bed stood his night horse already saddled. At the first low rumble, he came up into a sitting position and the end of his bed tarp flew back. With a single motion he jumped up, pulled on his boots, and made for his horse.

'Roll out, fellers!' he shouted. He swung into the saddle and turned his horse toward the noise. His call was unnecessary. Every man in camp knew the meaning of that rumbling sound. Bud West was crowding close to Banjy as he rode away, with old Meletone only a few paces behind, and others were hastily mounting. Nig poked his head from where he lay under the wagon, and the whites of his eyes gleamed in the pale moonlight. He peered at the cloud of dust arising in the wake of the running herd.

'Lawd, Lawd,' he murmured, ''t sounds lak ol' man thundah on the rampage and rollin' his watah kegs along ovah th' clouds. Ain't Ah glad Ah ain't no cowboy tonight!'

When he neared the lead, Banjy slowed down and started pressing against the left point. Bud West rode past him without checking speed.

'Hey, there!' yelled Banjy. 'Keep clear of the lead. Work on the point——' But his words were swallowed in the roar and confusion of the stampede.

When Sancho started running with the other cattle, he drove his way through them and led the way into a rocky draw. Brush crashed and loose rocks rattled behind as the main herd rolled forward. He darted out ahead and was thrown into a panic by a wild-riding man who dashed across his path and slapped him in the face with the tail of a slicker. Sancho plowed his feet into the ground trying to stop, but was bumped ahead by the pressure of cattle from the rear. He straightened up and hit his stride again, but he had covered only a short distance when another horse and rider plunged in front. This time a sharp report crashed at his eardrums and a blinding flash stung his eyes. A streak of flame spurted from the muzzle of a pistol and followed the bullet to where it dug itself into the ground at his feet. In spite of Banjy's warning, some of the men were risking themselves in front of the running cattle.

With slickers and pistol flashes slapping him in the face, Sancho slowed up and cattle breasted alongside him. The pressure of animals in his rear made it impossible for him to stop, and he turned aside. Thus the herd split into a huge Y, and Sancho led one point of it to the left. Another man rode down upon him and endeavored to turn him farther around. Sancho ducked behind this rider and plunged away at a sharp angle. Two animals followed him. The noise of the stampede was left behind and Sancho realized that he was getting nearer to freedom with each stride.

As he raced away to liberty, other cattle were making good their escape. After two hours the main bunches were brought together, and Banjy estimated they were five hundred head short.

'We cain't never get 'em all in the dark,' he said. He slipped his weight into his right stirrup and inspected his watch by the glow of his cigarette.

'We'll have to rap 'em hard and early in the mornin'.'

CHAPTER FIVE

NO WATER, NO GRASS

A FAINT glow burned itself into the eastern horizon. An owl sat upon the stub of a broken mesquite limb and watched the strange proceedings around him. He peered at a bright campfire and the coming daylight and gave a defiant hoot-hoot before flopping laboriously away to his hideout cave in the Red Bank bluffs. Old Meletone pushed his remuda into the corral and tied a rope across the gap. Walking to the fire and lighting a cigarette, he poured out a cup of coffee. He settled easily into a sitting position upon his crossed legs, and a smile flitted over his bronzed features while he watched the proficient Nig slapping the breakfast together.

Nig straightened up from his bending position over the fire and peered into the face of a huge silver watch. He verified the time by squinting wisely at the morning star which hung against the murky horizon. He next turned and appraised a mountainous pile of hot biscuits, a Dutch oven filled with layer upon layer of juicy steaks sizzling in a vat of brown gravy. Then he swung the pot of steaming coffee clear of the fire and ran his eye over the stack of empty plates and box of cutlery before he bawled out his famous breakfast call to the sleeping camp :

ROLL OUT, COWBOYS! ROLL OUT!
Chuck's all ready an' so's yer digger.
Biscuits foh de white folks an' con braid foh de niggah.
R-o-o-l-l ou-ou-ou-out — co-ow — boy-ees, ROLL OUT!

In the dusk of early morning the herd began to unwind itself from its bed ground and move away. The point drivers pressed hard against the leaders and filed them into a slender string between Banjy and Dave Houston, who were counting as they strung past. True to Banjy's estimate, they were more than five hundred head short.

Banjy recounted the tally knots as he untied them from his bridle rein. 'Did any of you fellers see Bill's one-horned dogy?' he asked, standing in his stirrups and scanning the herd that was now lengthening out into a trailing line. 'I didn't,' spoke up Bud West. 'And I don't think anybody else did since last night either. I'll bet he led the parade.'

'All right,' said Banjy, turning suddenly to the group of men. 'We've got to git them cattle back or know the reason why. Dave,' he ordered, 'you and three other men take this herd and keep it movin'. I'll take the rest of the outfit and swing back over the ground where we had our run last night and gather up them get-away cattle. I don't want to go off and leave five hundred, and if we don't git 'em today, we'll hold up till we do.'

Banjy scattered his men, and they combed over the high ridges and wide mesas where they knew cattle would be grazing early in the morning. By riding hard they covered a wide territory and gathered many of the lost steers. In mid-afternoon they caught up with the outfit and a recount showed them to be only three head short.

At that moment Sancho and his two followers were trailing down through the thick brush of a creek bottom. He had learned that by sticking to the brush he was safer from discovery and harder to drive out if discovered.

'We've been takin' it easy all day,' Dave Houston said to Banjy while the boss reclined against the wagon wheel after eating his belated noon meal. 'The herd is well filled up and rested. Must we drive out, or do you want to hang around some longer and look for them three lost steers?'

'We'd better drive,' Banjy replied. He stood up and looked back down the winding trail. 'There ain't no tellin' where we'd find 'em, and I hate to hold up any longer for just three head. They'll drift back toward home and some line rider'll shoo 'em along till they git across the river on our own range.'

A little twinkle came into his eyes and a ghost of a smile played over his weary countenance. 'I don't mind leavin' three steers this close to home, but I do hate for that pet steer of Bill's to be one of 'em. It cain't be helped, though. The Old Hoss'd have a fit if we lost any time lookin' for three head, that'll git home anyhow. We'll just hit the road and take Bill's gaff as it comes.'

Sancho followed his instinctive direction and worked back toward the land of his birth. He went unhurriedly, and a full week passed before he stood upon the north bank of the river and contemplated the stream of running water.

'Ho! little feller,' shouted Bill across the stream. 'I guess Banjy fooled hisself when he bragged that he'd land you in Kansas, eh, Bob?' He turned to Bob Long, who was helping him scout the north line for any animals Banjy might have lost.

'No, you're safe and sound for another year,' Bill continued. 'You git back where you belong and behave yo'rself,' he admonished as he urged Sancho into the water.

Bill Sanders chuckled with satisfaction. He watched Sancho splash his way across the river and lose himself in the brush of the opposite bank. Nor did Bill catch sight of him again that spring while he rode the range.

By the last part of April the Tree Top cattle had apparently settled themselves for a peaceful summer. Bill scattered the most of his men in line camps around the border of the range, and instructed them to turn back all animals that were inclined to stray from home. Under the blazing sun of May and June the early growth of grass withered and curled.

Only scattering showers fell in place of the customary rains, and before August water holes back in the heart of the range were drying up. More and more cattle were forced into the narrow strip of land which flanked the permanent water of the river. All grass along the river front shrunk away with startling rapidity as hungry mouths consumed it, and thousands of roaming hoofs cut the remaining blades into chaff and ground them into the dusty soil.

In their search for fresh grazing, cattle walked back as far from the trampled area as their strength permitted. Heavy clouds of dust floated aloft and marked their line of travel, while the long strings of miserable animals trailed to water and back again to the rolling hills, where shimmering heat waves raced over sun-parched ground.

Sancho's long legs and his reserve strength served him well. After drinking his fill of water, he did not lie upon the river bank and rest like most cattle, but instead he turned at once and with bulging sides started back for grass. His easy stride carried him far into the foothills beyond the distance that ordinary steers could travel. Here, he found the best grazing and retained most of his strength because of it.

On the other hand, the weak cattle suffered most from their handicap of limited travel, and they steadily became weaker. The mother cows and their calves were drooping under the strain, the mothers failing because the suckling calves were draining away their strength, and the calves failing because their mother's emaciated condition curtailed their milk supply. An omen of ruin hovered over the Tree Top outfit.

The Old Hoss had gone north a month after Banjy left. His plan was to meet the herd at destination and sell it, and then take a vacation in the East. He had not returned, and the anguish of watching the Tree Top cattle wither and starve fell to Bill Sanders.

Early in July Bill mailed a letter to him, but no answer came back, and Bill spent many anxious hours of divided time, waiting to hear from the Old Hoss and hoping for rain as he watched the scattered clouds drifting high overhead. When he at last despaired, he determined to take matters into his own hands and try to avert the impending disaster.

Bob Long and a newly hired man named Steve Barr were the only two men at the headquarter ranch with Bill. Bob was supposed to be breaking out the year's crop of young horses, but under the handicap of driving all saddle stock five miles to water and back each day, he went about his principal task in a mood of indifference. Steve Barr put in most of his time cooking and trying to coax enough water for house use from the failing well. The two cowboys exchanged glances when on the last day of August Bill Sanders called them out of bed at four o'clock in the morning, and ordered them to bring in all saddle horses while he prepared breakfast.

After breakfast Bill pushed his chair from the table, cocked it on the two rear legs, and stared thoughtfully at the wall lamp where it cast its dim light.

'These cattle are starvin', and we've got to do somethin' about it,' he said simply.

A wreath of a grin played across Bob Long's face as he leaned back and blew a thin string of smoke toward the ceiling. 'I guess they're starvin' all right, but I cain't see what we can do about it,' he hedged. 'We cain't make it rain, and that's about the only thing that will help us.'

'No, we cain't make it rain,' Bill agreed patiently, 'and a rain wouldn't take care of everything anyhow. It's too late to grow a crop of grass this year.' Bill let his tilted chair fall to the floor and rest on its four legs. An earnest look came into his eyes while he toyed with an empty coffee cup. 'What we need,' he said, 'is grass. These cows have got to have grass — and there's grass somewhere——'

'A rain wouldn't hurt us none,' argued Bob. 'We've got some grass back in the hills —— What we need is water back there.'

'We might pray a little,' suggested Steve Barr. 'When I was a kid and went to Sunday School, they always told me that faith would move mountains.'

Bill Sanders permitted Bob's chuckle to die out and then struck the table sharply with his open hand. 'Now, listen!' he commanded. 'Listen to me. Since you mention about movin' a mountain, I'd like to know if either one of you fellers ever heard of a man named Mohamet and a mountain, when one or the other had to be moved. No? Well, it don't make no difference. You're goin' to hear somethin' else now!'

Bill dipped a match stub into the dregs of his coffee cup, and with the wet tip traced a line upon the oilcloth table cover. The line swung slightly southeast and then turned to the west. 'This,' he said, 'takes in a scope of country around on the San Saba, the Llanos, and Devils River and up the Pecos divide.'

He redipped the match, and traced another line directly toward the west and bent it around in a southwesterly direction until the point of it came almost in contact with the first line. 'This,' he explained, 'takes in the mouth of the Kickapoo, the two Conchos, and back around to the Pecos divide. There's water in all this country, but I don't know about grass. I aim for you two fellers to hit the trail and find out in short order!'

'I guess you aim for us to sprout wings and fly a little,' drawled Steve. 'I know that country, and it ain't but about five hundred miles around them little lines you've drawed——'

'Don't waste no time arguin' about it,' interrupted Bill. 'There's plenty hossflesh on this ranch, and when that's gone we'll git more. You fellers go out to that corral and get a couple of good, strong ponies and a light pack outfit apiece and ride away.

'Steve,' Bill went on sharply, retracing his first line, 'you follow Battle Creek down to its mouth on the San Saba and then hit across for the Llanos and on around. Bob, you take the west route. Cross over the Kickapoo and onto the Concho. If either of you find grass and water together — grab onto it — and you'd better not come back till you do find somethin',' he finished with finality.

'How about the north and east?' Bob asked, rolling a slicker around a small bundle of provisions. 'It always rains more in them directions than it does in the west or south, and maybe we could find somethin' there.'

'It ain't no use to go east,' replied Bill. 'The farmers are comin' into that country thicker than jack rabbits and they've got the cowmen crowded out. Banjy'll be back in the next ten or fifteen days, and if there's any grass in the north, he'll know about it.'

Bill arose and placed one foot in the bottom of his chair. He leaned over the table and peered earnestly at the two men, who were now silenced in preparations for their trip.

'Remember, boys, this is serious. You fellers roll yo'r dough, ride hard, and hurry back. While you're gone, I'll be whippin' things into shape around here, and the next day after we locate some range we'll have these Tree Top cows steppin' toward it.'

CHAPTER SIX
'IT'S GOT TO BE DONE!'

A WEEK later Bill stood at the horse corral and watched a rider with a lead horse coming over the hill from the south. The rider was Steve Barr. He reported to Bill that he had found some unappropriated range, but the country was filling up so fast with other drouth-stricken cattle that he doubted the widsom of moving into it for the winter. Two days later Bob Long returned and made a report of his findings.

'I found lots of water and grass,' Bob said. 'But I'm afraid it won't do us no good.'

'Why not?' Bill asked.

'Well, it's this way,' resumed Bob unhurriedly. 'I rode up the South Concho to its headwaters. There's plenty of water, but not enough grass to keep a prairie dog alive. I camped there one night and met up with an old trapper who had been clean from the Rio Grande to the New Mexico line and back around the foot of the plains in his trappin' expeditions. He told me there wasn't a bite of grass anywhere except out on the Pecos.'

'Well, sir,' continued Bob. 'I lit a shuck out across that divide for the Pecos and me and my two ponies mighty nigh kicked the bucket. If I hadn't run across a squatter out there with a pore little weak well with jus' about enough water for a good healthy goose — we'd've dried up and blowed away like a tree leaf after frost hits it. That there little well has got ever' bit of water there is for a hundred miles between the Concho and Pecos Rivers.'

Bob paused in his recital long enough to roll another of his inevitable cigarettes. Steve twisted his back and slid himself around the corral fence corner, keeping up with the travel of the shade. Bill stabbed a small stick with the point of his open knife blade and stood up. He walked around in a short circle and came to a stop directly in front of Bob.

'The old Circle Bar outfit,' continued Bob, as he snorted a column of smoke from each nostril, 'has got an outfit that's made for our needs just like a boot made to fit yo'r foot. There's a little more'n a hundred sections of it. She straddles the river for forty miles and controls all outdoors. A drouth run all the cattle out of the country two years ago and it ain't been restocked yet. Grass is half stirrup high as far back from the river as a cow can travel.'

'Did you make any kind of deal to tie it up?' Bill asked.

'No,' said Bob thoughtfully. 'That place is a leetle bit too far from taw for me. I thought I'd better tell you about it first.'

During the short silence that followed, Bill Sanders walked past the corral gate, turned, and stopped abruptly. He let his gaze wander over the countryside of wilted tree leaves and parched grass. He looked at a long string of dust-covered cattle, topping a hill, winding silently toward the river five miles away. He then directed his gaze toward his two companions.

'I ain't afraid to tie that grass up,' he said, with his jaws snapping shut. 'You fellers run in the saddle hosses and catch old Spindleshanks and Monkey Face for me. They're the best travelers in my string. While you're doin' that, I'll be rolling my slicker and a little grub together. I aim to see that Pecos grass and tie it up inside of three days.'

Bill threw the lead rope of the pack horse over his shoulder and prepared to mount. He then turned sharply to Bob Long.

'How many unbroke ponies have we got that you can fan out and make ready for work in the next three weeks?'

'Well,' replied Bob thoughtfully, looking at the ground and making marks in the dust with the toe of his boot and mumbling more to himself than aloud. 'I've already rode out twenty-five head of four-year-olds. They're all pretty good now. There's five more on stake that's been rode a couple of saddles apiece. They'll be all right too. There's ten more four-year-olds that ain't been touched; and then there's about twenty more head of overgrowed three-year-olds that's big enough to carry a man part of a day — if I just had time enough to do all this.'

Bill Sanders stood by the side of his horse with one foot in the stirrup, looking at Bob Long and straining his ears to catch the mumbled words.

'About sixty more head of broncs could be slapped into shape,' Bob spoke up, raising his head and looking at Bill. 'About half of 'em will be kind of raw and hard to navigate. Three weeks ain't much time for a feller to thrash out a bunch of broncs by hisself.'

Bill removed his foot from the stirrup and turned to face the bronc buster.

'I don't like to take any of the men away from the line camps at this time,' he said, slapping his boot top with a bridle rein. 'But I'll tell you what. You hustle around and pick up a couple of bronc-twisters to help you out, and get as many of them young ponies broke as you can.'

'That's the hot stuff,' rejoined Bob with the first show of interest. 'When me and a couple of other twisters git lined out on them broncos, we'll make the fur fly like a cat's claws on a rabbit.'

'Hold up, there!' Bill admonished. 'Don't be too rough on 'em. There ain't never been any Tree Top ponies butchered up yet, and I don't want it to start now. But you don't have to waste any time breakin' 'em dog-gentle. Jus' break 'em to stand on stake and make 'em good hackamore wise. That will be enough. It won't hurt any if they do buck a little on a cold mornin'. Them cowpunchers'll need somethin' like that to settle their breakfast anyhow.'

'All right,' laughed Bob, 'but I pity the cowhand that draws a full string of them raw broncs. He'll have his hands full all the time without doin' any work.'

'Don't worry about that,' Bill said. 'We won't mount any one man on raw ponies altogether. We'll scatter 'em out and make ever' man take his share. From the work starin' us in the face, a burro is liable to look good to a Tree Top man before it's all over with.'

With those last words, Bill swung into his saddle. 'Adios,' he said, and he turned his horse and rode away.

Seven days later at noon Bill returned after an all night's ride. His lips were cracked and bleeding from long hours exposed to blistering wind and sun. His two horses were footsore and sweat-caked, and resembled walking skeletons of wasted horseflesh. As he walked stiff-legged around the corral, the Old Hoss came driving up in his buggy. The haggard expression upon his face matched the travel-worn countenance of Bill Sanders.

'This is a fine mess we're into,' were his words of greeting. 'Why in thunder did you let things get in this shape? I never thought you'd sit around and let these cattle starve and not say a word about it to anybody,' he finished with mounting anger.

Bill opened his bloodshot eyes, and his jaw dropped in amazement while he strove to keep down his own temper at the unjust criticism.

'Don't go too fast,' he said evenly. 'I ain't got no control over the weather, and if you'll just look at the date on that letter I wrote you'll have to own that I sent word in plenty of time. You didn't send me no word of any kind and didn't come back, so I done the best I could. Anyhow, I ain't exactly been settin' around here twiddlin' my thumbs.'

'Oh,' said the Old Hoss, 'I guess I spoke too quick. I didn't get any letter. What do you figure on doing?'

'I've found some grass,' Bill said simply, 'and I'm getting ready to drive to it.'

'Good!' exclaimed the Old Hoss. 'I knew you'd do something. Where is the grass and when do we start?'

'Hold up a minute,' said Bill grimly. 'Don't let yo'rself git too roused up about this thing till you hear all the particulars. There's plenty of grass all right and it's a regular paradise to winter in, but there's one big horsefly in the ointment. It's located out on the Pecos River, and before we can get the Tree Top cattle to it, we'll have to make a hundred-mile drive without water.'

The Old Hoss again let his face go blank and resume its haggard expression. Then he blazed forth in sudden anger.

'Why, Bill,' he sputtered, 'you've surely lost your senses. Don't you know better than to try anything like that? These cattle aren't a bunch of dry-land lizards.'

Bill again fought to control his temper and turned to face him. 'There ain't no use to quarrel about it now,' he said. 'We've got to do it. I've already tied up the deal and drawed a sight draft against you for a thousand dollars for an option to run thirty days. The balance of fourteen thousand dollars will be due when we get the first cattle there.'

The Old Hoss turned and started to unharness his team. When this was completed, he seemed under better control.

'Forgive me, Bill,' he said. 'I shouldn't have lost my temper. I know you're interested in these cattle as much as I am. I know you acted for what you thought was best. I appreciate your interest, but this won't do. It's out of the question to drive these cattle a hundred miles without water. We'll never have to pay the balance of that money because we'll never get the cattle there. I'll just charge off that thousand dollars and forget about it.' Without another word he turned decisively and strode into the ranch house. Bill turned in the opposite direction, and stood leaning against the corral fence with his arms hooked over the top rail.

'Ever'thing has gone to hell in a hand-basket, Bob,' Bill said hopelessly to the bronco breaker. 'The Old Hoss spilled water in our powder and we're plumb out of ammunition. It looks like I've throwed away a thousand dollars of his money, and I guess I'm just about slated to roll my bed and look for another job.'

Nothing more than the barest words to make up common-place conversation had passed between the Old Hoss and Bill up to bedtime. With the brand of weariness and uncertainty stamped heavily upon his face, the Old Hoss retired soon after darkness without voicing the least hint of his intentions. In a wild desire to be alone with his thoughts, Bill walked outside the yard to fight out his problem.

He was compelled to admit that his future was far from promising. The Old Hoss had said he would overlook the thou-sand-dollar loss — and Bill knew he would — but he would never forget it. Bill knew that as long as he stayed on the Tree Top Ranch he would be just another cowhand. Never again would the Old Hoss place confidence in him as he had in the past. He smiled bitterly at the thought that he would never lose another thousand dollars. From now on he would not be authorized to draw a check even for five dollars.

The thoughts of Virginia Lowe that had annoyed Bill now changed to sadness. He had often let his imagination run, and picture a time in the future where they might be thrown together under happier circumstances. But now —? He realized that he had just as well forget. He would never have the face to see her again after his failure. He smiled bitterly to himself. He had lost his standing with the Old Hoss, but he still retained his discretion, and no one shared the secret of his cherished thoughts.

Then Bill thought of Banjy, and was reminded that he was due back at the ranch any time now, and he wondered what the wise old trail man would think of his — as Meletone would say — fiasco. In spite of the Old Hoss and his strong opinion against it,

Bill still believed his scheme was sound — but he would never have a chance to prove it. That is, unless — unless, Banjy——

Bill was interrupted in his meditation by the distant rumble of many horses traveling. His straining ears picked out the cluck-cluck of rolling wagon wheels — the subdued voices of men and the jingle of a saddle horse bell.

'Banjy!' he shouted with pure joy. Banjy would have something to say. Banjy would know the answer.

The four-horse team swung around to the side gate of the yard and came to a stop. Nig plumped heavily from the wagon seat, and Bill strained his eyes to pick out Banjy in the swarm of horsemen who were spreading around the spot and dismounting. Paying scant heed to greetings of others, Bill rushed up to the heavy-bodied trail man and grasped his hand.

'You're good for sore eyes,' he said eagerly. 'I'd rather see you right now than any other person in the world.'

'I've cut the dirt of a lot of dry trail to get here,' said Banjy wearily, leaning against a gatepost. 'I had to, or my saddle ponies would've starved to death. You're about dried up and blowed away too. What in the Sam Hill are we goin' to do?'

'I'm goin' to talk to you,' Bill replied with finality.

Until late that night, Bill and Banjy sat outside near the corral while Bill unfolded his plan. Ere long Banjy's sharp eyes were sparkling with interest that matched the glow from the tip of his cigarette. At last they came to an understanding, and next morning they stood firmly against the strong opinions of the Old Hoss in an argument which lasted most of the day.

'There's no use to talk any more,' the Old Hoss said doggedly. 'It can't be done.'

'It's got to be done,' flung back Banjy, taking the lead. 'It may never have been done before, but we're goin' to start out and make some history ourselves.'

'Yes,' replied the Old Hoss with bitter satire, 'we'll make history all right, but it will be recorded that a weak old man let two misguided cowboys talk him into the notion of driving out a string of cattle that starved to death for water on the way.'

'What's the difference?' flung back Banjy, as he lit another cigarette and sucked deep drafts of smoke into his lungs. 'If they don't die on the way to the Pecos, they'll die on the Tree Top range like minnows in a mudhole. You know it's out of the question to winter here. There won't be a hundred cattle alive next spring.'

The Old Hoss remained silent. Taking advantage of this moment of indecision, Banjy hurried to press his point.

'You know we cain't hope for anything on the Llanos and the Devil's River country. From what the boys say that country will be packed full of cattle before spring. You know that the worst thing a feller can do is to overstock. In my time I've seen a drouth like this one, now and then, and I've seen the time when men was foolish enough to crowd a range. Old Mother Nature won't stand for any such monkey business, and a big die-up always follows overstockin'.'

The Old Hoss remained silent and unmoved in a deep study. Bill Sanders was slicing shavings from a small stick in his hand, but his eyes held a gleam of satisfaction.

'As far as I'm concerned,' resumed Banjy, 'the Pecos is the only way out for us. Instead of settin' here arguin' about it, you'd better thank yo'r Maker that Bill had sense enough to spend a thousand dollars for the option on that grass. I ain't no gambler like some in this outfit, but I'd be willin' to risk a hundred dollars that you can sell that option right now for a nice profit. This drouth is bad,' he continued, leaning forward and pounding an open palm with a closed fist. 'I've rode through it all the way from Red River to here, and I know what I'm talkin' about.'

The Old Hoss raised his eyes and looked at the two men in front of him. He cleared his throat, drew a long breath, and said: 'Now let me talk awhile. A herd of cattle will never make it over that divide. The weakest ones will drop out on the trail and die like flies after frost time. The stronger ones will go desert-crazed and scatter all over the country until they die too.'

'Not by a long shot,' replied Bill Sanders, with a tone of conviction in his voice. 'I went over ever' foot of ground myself. It's only thirty miles from headwaters on the Concho to the top of the divide. From there, the Centralia draw heads off and runs almost straight to the Pecos. Our herds'll make that first thirty miles O.K. without losin' their heads. When they once get started down the Centralia, they'll stay in it. Cattle always go downhill when they're huntin' for water, and the thirstier they get the closer they'll stick to that draw.'

Bill paused with a glance at his two listeners. He felt encouraged at Banjy's nod of approval and his contented manner of puffing on his cigarette. The Old Hoss remained silent and chewed the corner of his mustache.

'Our biggest job,' resumed Bill, 'will be holdin' them cattle back. If the wind is in their faces, they can smell water for thirty or forty miles and we'll have to do some tall and fancy ridin' in the lead to keep 'em from runnin' their fool heads off.'

'But how about the men and horses?' objected the Old Hoss. 'Even if I own up that cattle can go a week or ten days without water — men and horses can't.'

'We've got you stopped on that one too,' countered Banjy. 'It won't be a week. When we start a herd away from the Concho water, we'll keep 'em drillin' till we land on the Pecos. The barrel in the chuck wagon will hold enough for drinkin' and a little cookin'. There ain't goin' to be anybody loafin' around camp. Them wagon wheels will be kept rollin' and them cowhands will have to pound the leather of their saddles day and night.'

Banjy glanced over to the hill where old Meletone was starting the saddle horses to water on the river five miles away — two hundred and fifty head of fine saddle stock gaunted from scarcity of grass and water.

'As for the hosses,' he said, 'instead of swappin' in midstream — as a feller says — we'll swap on top of the divide. We'll leave half of the *remuda* on water with two men. When the herd is about halfway over, they can make a hard night drive and catch us at daylight. We'll change then and send our thirsty ponies on ahead to the Pecos.'

'Some scheming. Some scheming,' the Old Hoss commented dryly. 'If I was inclined to be suspicious, I'd think you fellows had been talking behind my back. But I've got another question for you,' he continued, raising his eyes. 'How do you fellows propose to hold these cattle this winter — that is, if you get them there? You won't have any neighbors to help ride line and they'll scatter all over Hades. You won't gather half of them next spring.'

'That won't bother any,' rejoined Bill. 'Me and Banjy can pitch our camps on the river fifty miles apart. We'll keep men to ride line twenty miles back from the river on both sides. When spring comes, we'll have ever' one right in our pockets.'

'But we'll have neighbors,' Banjy reminded. 'Before thirty days is up we'll be ridin' high, wide, and handsome to keep other fellers' stock off our range. This drouth is a stem-winder, and before spring that country out there will fill up with cattle like Nig sifts flour in his bread pan.'

'All right. All right,' acquiesced the Old Hoss, his expression indicating that he had come to a final decision. 'Stop puffing away at me and give me a little breathing-spell. If the scheme fails, we'll all go down together. I'll be broke and a couple of fancy cowhands will be hunting a job. And,' he continued, 'since we all understand each other, you fellows can handle things your own way. I'll just hang around in case I'm needed. You both know how to draw checks, and don't try to shave expenses too much. It's going to be a hard grind, and I want my men to have the best.'

The Old Hoss arose and started away. He turned and again faced his two men. 'I just want to say,' he said slowly, 'if you fellows scratch out of this one — my hat is off to you, Bill Sanders.'

CHAPTER SEVEN
BIG ROUND-UP

I N A SHORT time after the Old Hoss assented to the plans the Tree Top headquarters hummed, with Banjy in active command.

'We've got about fifteen thousand cattle to move,' he said by way of computation. 'We can make 'em up in four herds of about thirty-five hundred head each. I want Bill to handle the first one that's ready to go. It's his plan, and I want him to have credit for it. If it fails, his shoulders are big enough to tote the blame.'

'That's satisfactory to me,' agreed the Old Hoss. 'It's all up to you and Bill.'

'All right,' replied Banjy, turning to Bill. 'You take the first herd out as quick as we can gather it. I'll follow with the second and Dave Houston can bring the third.' Then, as Banjy hesitated, the Old Hoss arose with quick decision upon his face.

'You said there'd be four herds. I guess you're looking for another trail boss. Just to show you fellers that I'm still in the game I'll bring out that fourth herd myself.'

'Good!' exclaimed Banjy. 'I knew you'd line up with us.'

'Now, then,' continued Banjy. 'Each man will stop his herd on the Concho headwaters and rest for a full day. After the herd is filled up, he'll start his dash at high noon and not stop until he gets to Pecos water. Bill can stay with his herd and get 'em scattered out on the new range. He can then receive all other cattle as fast as they arrive. I'll turn my herd over to Bill when I get there, and then I'll come back to the Concho and relieve you.'

As preparations for the gigantic undertaking proceeded, Bill's heart warmed toward the Old Hoss. The old man threw his full support to the program, and busied himself with routine details for which neither Bill nor Banjy had time or inclination to bother about. Bill felt a little twinge of pity as he noted how the troubled old fellow came to lean upon his men. He made no secret of the comfort he derived in having such tried and trusted ones about him.

He showed plainly how he relied upon the wise and loyal counsel of good old Banjy, so rich in his store of cattle knowledge. Bill knew that the Old Hoss was offering proof of his confidence and was endeavoring to atone for his earlier doubts when he consented for him to drive the first herd. The Old Hoss showed his pride in the faithful Nig and wise old Meletone, who saw much and said little, in the quick-tempered Dave Houston, who asked favors from no man; in the daring Bob Long, who risked life and limb in his task of breaking out wild horses for use later on. Bill could see that the Old Hoss had a certain admiration for the garrulous and irresponsible Bud West, who never appeared to have a serious thought and who was ready to laugh at fate and willing to risk a wager on the turn of life's events, and all the others upon whom he now depended to play a part in the attempt to save his fortune from threatened disaster.

Banjy assumed responsibility of conditioning all equipment and securing the necessary supplies. He dispatched teamsters to Coleman Town to freight out stores of provisions and other necessities. He hired extra men and set them to mending harness, outfitting chuck wagons, shoeing horses, making rope corrals, and all other details in the scheme of preparation.

To Bill Sanders fell the job of concentrating all saddle and work animals and redistributing them. When he made an assignment of horses to each man, he was careful to allot a share of the young animals that Bob Long and his helpers were breaking in.

Standing together one morning, Bill and Banjy were looking over a bunch of twenty young horses that Bob and one of his men were driving into the corral for another riding.

'Too bad,' said Bill, with a shake of his head, as he noted fresh cinch sores where tightened girths had cut into their bodies and the peeling streaks of skin on their noses from hackamore burns. 'Too bad to have nice young ponies scarred up that way. We ain't never treated a Tree Top horse like that before and I hate to see it done now. I'm afraid Bob is a little too rough.'

'Yep,' replied Banjy with a smile, 'but you dished out the powders yo'rself. You told 'im to produce saddle hoss flesh from raw material and to do it in a hurry. A feller cain't handle broncs very easy when he's tryin' to turn 'em out wholesale style. The way him and them two broncoderos are tearin' at them wild ponies, it's a wonder they ain't killed a dozen or so by now——.'

A stampede of hoofs accompanied by roars of shouts and laughter drowned out Banjy's words. He and Bill turned toward the corral where sat some eight or ten cowboys perched upon the top rail. Between the gate wings, with one of Bob's new men aboard, was a wild horse, wiping up the ground in his efforts to unseat the rider.

'Whoo-ee!' shouted Dave Houston from his perch. 'Watch 'im go! He's a salty dog that's huntin' for meat. Watch 'im buck! He can sunfish and crawfish in the same jump. That there mustang has got hisself rolled into a knot and is bouncin' around like a rubber ball.'

'I say, watch that peeler ride!' answered Bud West. 'He's scratchin' that bronc's hide from throat-latch to tail. I bet he could ride a streak of greased lightnin' if he could git his saddle on it. Boy! How I wish I could set a hoss like that! I wouldn't do nothin' but show off before all the gals.'

'How do you like that for bronc peelin'?' asked Bob, riding up to Bill and Banjy.

'He's about as clean a setter as I ever saw,' admitted Bill. 'Where did you catch 'im? I don't ever remember seein' 'im in the country anywhere. He looks like a Mexican.'

'He's a Mexican, all right,' Bob replied. 'Just started to work yesterday. He comes from southern Texas and he's a *puro vaquero*. Says he used to work for a feller down there named Harte. The Mexicans all call 'im Harte-Corazon. The *corazon* means heart in Spanish——'

'Cora—— Hell's bells!' exclaimed Banjy. 'Ben Harte. How well I happen to know that gent — and just a little piece of advice to you for the good of us all — you'd better get rid of that *hombre* in a hurry. He ain't here for no good to us.'

At Bill Sanders's and Bob Long's look of inquiry, Banjy explained: 'Ben Harte — the feller he calls Corazon — is the biggest cow thief that ever sun-fished out of a noose. He's got that Mexican up here to spy out the lay of the land. The first thing we know, we'll be losin' cattle in droves. I don't want any of Ben Harte's outfit mixed up with this one.'

'You needn't be uneasy about this feller,' Bob assured them. 'He hates Harte wuss'n you hate a rattlesnake. Says he had to run off without his pay to keep Harte from killin' 'im. Says Harte's *muy malo*.'

'I guess you'd call 'im bad,' Banjy laughed. 'There's been more'n one man that never got out of them Nueces canyons where Harte's ranch is, after he learnt too much or got too much wages comin' to 'im. Harte's mighty tough on Mexicans. I don't see why any of 'em ever stay around 'im, but they do, and they seem to think he's a little tin god.'

'This boy says Harte's got some mighty fine hosses,' Bob stipulated.

'Yes,' Banjy admitted. 'That's the only decent thing about 'im. He does raise good hosses, and trains 'em for cow ponies too. He claims to have a strain of the old Arabian ponies that the Spaniards brought to this country more'n three hundred years ago. They're the toughest and wildest of any breed I ever saw. That accounts for this boy's good ridin'. If he stayed around Harte, he had to be a clean setter to stick on them ponies.'

The bronco had stopped his bucking, and went scampering away in a run with another rider hazing him along. Banjy took a close look at the *vaquero* as he passed, and shook his head. 'Never saw that feller before,' he admitted. 'Guess he come to Harte after I left the country.'

Banjy turned again to his listeners. 'Harte brands his cows with a big heart on the left side about the same place where we put the Tree Top. He brands his ponies the deuce of hearts — a little one on the left thigh and shoulder. I never knowed of 'im stealin' a hoss, but he could shore drag in the cattle. About ten years ago I worked for the Door Key outfit that joined 'im on the north. He just about stole us blind. We got the Rangers on his trail and they killed off some of his men and put Harte in the Pen. They tell me he's out now. That sort of broke 'im up in business for a while, but I heard last year that he's about to git back on his feet agin.'

'Shore, I remember now,' said Bill Sanders. 'I heard about that feller with his *remuda* of deuce-of-hearts ponies. He drove a herd up the trail last spring. Well, I don't care much what he does down on the Nueces, but him and them brush hands of his'n had better keep their ropes off the Tree Top dogies.'

And with that the subject of Ben Harte was dropped while the two men busied themselves with the problem at hand.

The day before the great Tree Top round-up was to start, it rained. Not a mere sprinkle, but, as Bud West expressed it, 'a regular hell-quencher.' Far back in the ranges where grass had been untouched by cattle for months, the creeks and water holes were full to the brim. It was now apparent that part of the cattle could be wintered at home, and this called for a hasty revision of the plans.

Upon advice of Bill Sanders and Banjy, the Old Hoss decided to keep the weakened mother cows and their young calves at home and move only the stout, dry cattle. And now the four herds could be cut to three of about thirty-seven hundred head. Then, as the weather cleared and the muddy ground settled into firmness, every available Tree Top man and horse was pressed relentlessly into service.

Bill Sanders led a crew of fifteen men to the western edge of the range and struck the first blow against the impending disaster when he made a round-up and gathered more than five hundred dry cattle. Banjy headed a similar outfit that swung around to the east, and Dave Houston with a crew of day herders to hold cattle from Bill's and Banjy's round-ups was thrown to the center. After the first day the two range bosses were pouring cattle into Dave's herd by the hundreds.

Three days later Bill Sanders rode at the head of five hundred steers, heifers, and dry cows. He stopped his horse on the brink of Dove Creek Basin and felt a thrill of pride as he viewed the panorama before him. It had been a long time since Bill had seen Tree Top cattle contented.

But now, back on the upper prongs of Dove Creek, where the scarcity of water had spared the old grass, were hundreds upon hundreds of cattle quietly grazing. From rim to rim they stretched, and at intervals scattered along each divide he could see Dave Houston's men holding the grazing animals in shape. A mile down the creek three men were letting the lead cattle gently down to water. Half a mile back up the draw two drag drivers were bringing up laggards to this monstrous herd. Sitting in the shade of a tree not far from him were Dave Houston and the Old Hoss, conferring over a small notebook.

'How many you got, Dave?' Bill asked, as he rode up.

'We're just figuring up,' smiled the Old Hoss. 'All these figures make me feel kind of important anyway.' Then he grew serious. 'From our figures this last bunch of yours makes a little better than thirty-seven hundred head. Banjy will be ready with another bunch tonight, but you won't need them.'

'No,' replied Bill thoughtfully, 'I guess I've just about got my cargo and it's time to move'; and turning to Dave Houston: 'Drift 'em out onto the brushy flats, Dave. I'll get my outfit in shape and take 'em off yo'r hands tonight. When the first crow flops his wings in the mornin' my wagon wheels will roll toward the west and we'll be on our way.'

'You'll have to go off without yo'r little one-horned Sancho steer,' remarked Dave. 'I've had 'im a couple of times since we started out, but he give me the slip. He's snaky, and we've been holdin' this herd too loose for a foxy steer.'

'Oh, well,' replied Bill, 'there'll be other round-ups, and somebody'll hang onto 'im before the work is over with. He cain't get away ever' time.'

Out on the brushy flats where Bill held his herd there came the first streaks of dawn. Along with the coming day arose a low rumble increasing in volume ; the concerted tap of hoofs ; the clash of horns — feet raking across the ground, soft coughs and sneezes, multiplied countless times as thirty-seven hundred cattle stirred themselves and arose from their bed ground. They gained their feet and moved away in one direction, their close formation presenting a solid, moving wall across their front like the roll of a misty cloud.

Silent men, with their bearded faces blurred in the dark shadows of early morning and with eyes shining eagerly through the dusk, rode clear-footed horses back and forth along the mass of packed cattle, pressing them into a trailing line. As the herd lengthened out and hit the swing of the trail, Bill Sanders left it and returned to camp.

The last guard had finished their breakfast upon his arrival and were now saddling day horses. Old Meletone was busy coiling up the ropes of this dismantled corral. The loose saddle horses were spreading out in fan shape, grazing slowly in the direction of the headquarters ranch. Nig was pushing the last of his smoke-blackened pots into the rawhide 'possum sack where it swung underneath the wagon bed. Bud West, whom Bill had named as wagon pilot, stood patiently at the head of the six-horse team. The Old Hoss held the lines of his buggy team and stood ready to mount into the vehicle. Bill saw him looking wistfully over the trampled ground at his feet. There were scraps of discarded food, a crushed coffee package, an empty tobacco sack, the frayed end of a broken rope, and a mound of white ashes — the things that within the next few minutes would mark an abandoned camp site.

Bill stood beside Bud West, and with outstretched arm pointed out distant landmarks that were to guide him to the next camp spot, and as he dropped his arm and pulled his horse back a step from the lead team, things began to move.

First came Nig, swelling with pride at his part of the program as he climbed to the seat of his chuck wagon. He gathered up the intricate assembly of lines and snapped them over the backs of the six-horse team. The eager horses responded and lunged into their collars. The heavy wagon, groaning under its load of provision and equipment, clucked sharply as it gained speed, and went careening down the trail close on the heels of Bud West's galloping horse. Old Meletone swung the lash of his long whip with severity, whipping a lagging *remuda* into line behind the swaying wagon. Bill smiled as he watched Nig bouncing clear of the spring seat, rearing back on the lines, steadying the plunging horses while the wagon bumped over rough ground. Then Bill turned to the Old Hoss.

'We'll git there,' Bill said softly. 'Don't you go to worryin' and losin' sleep about this herd. You study about gettin' them others started before they gobble up all the feed away from the cows and calves.'

'You're worrying more than I am,' smiled the Old Hoss with moist eyes. 'I know you'll get there, but I hate to see you go off without me or Banjy with you. But I think you'd better be going now.' He turned away quickly to hide his emotion.

Bill mounted and rode after the long herd, which was now stretched out for two miles, swinging around hill points and topping the low hogbacks of the lower Concho as it made its way out into the unknown.

CHAPTER EIGHT

A PRICKLY PEAR FEAST

THE herd that Bill Sanders drove away had been made ready in a record short time. Both he and Banjy grabbed up cattle at the rate of more than a thousand head a day and turned them over to Dave Houston. After Bill had gone, and with only Banjy's outfit working full time, the second one was much slower. Nevertheless, a week later saw another herd gathered to full strength and Banjy directing it up the trail laid out by Bill Sanders. The Old Hoss and Dave Houston exercised joint authority over the last outfit, and the Old Hoss insisted upon cleaning the range of every dry animal that was able to walk. Therefore the riders swept back and forth over the range time and again until he was satisfied.

The last night, the Old Hoss bedded his herd at what he was pleased to call 'The Bill Sanders Camp.' At midnight he lay awake gazing at the starry heavens when the distant tramp of a horse's feet stirred him from his reverie. The horse was not ridden by one of the guard men, he knew, for the herd lay in the opposite direction. As the sound drew nearer and the hoof-beats became plainer, he guessed from the slow and regular tread that the animal making them was tired. Then the horse broke into a gallop, and simultaneously came the whistled bars of a rollicking tune. A glow of excitement flowed through him. He knew of but one man who whistled that tune. It was Bud West. Bud had gone with Bill Sanders. Within a few short moments he would have news.

Bud rode into camp, loosed his girth, and dropped the saddle to the ground with a dull thud. He removed the bridle from his horse and swished the animal with the tip end of the reins, which sent him toward the tinkling bell in the *remuda*. As he approached the smouldering campfire, men arose from their beds and gathered around him.

'That's the way to act,' said Bud. 'Git up and pay tribute to a returned hero.'

'But tell us about the trip,' insisted the Old Hoss. 'How far have you come today?'

'I've come from the Pecos,' said Bud wearily, 'and if you fellers think it ain't a long jump, just try it some time. I had a fresh hoss staked out at the nester's on the divide or I never would've made it.'

'But how about the herd?' persisted the Old Hoss. 'Did you make it all right?'

'Make it?' repeated Bud with importance. 'Of course we made it. We already had it made before we started. We strung them dogies over that divide like a swarm of bees on the move, and we never lost a head.'

'Gaw! Gaw!' coughed Dave Houston. 'You make me tired — comin' in here in the middle of the night and wakin' ever'body up to tell us somethin' we already knew. You blow around like you had somethin' to do with gettin' that herd across. You couldn't drive a gentle milk cow down a lane to water.'

'Just the same, *amigo*,' Bud said as he drained the remains of coffee from the pot into a cup, 'I'm ready to back myself with dough. I've got money that says I can run rings around you in anythin' you want to start.'

The Old Hoss sighed with relief at Bud's account of the trip to the Pecos. He then lapsed into silence, but was aroused by what appeared to be the starting of a quarrel.

'Enough of that,' he said crisply. 'You fellows go to bed and sleep it over. You'll feel better tomorrow.'

'All right,' mumbled Bud as he crawled into an empty bed belonging to one of the men on guard. 'But any time that swell-head over there thinks he's got anythin' on me, I'm ready to make a showdown.'

Sancho had been caught in the round-ups many times and turned into the day herd, but it was easy for him to get away whenever the spirit moved him. When the Old Hoss handed down his edict that the range be cleaned of all dry cattle, Sancho met with firmer opposition. He found that it had become very difficult for him to make his escape in the daytime. His unruly ways had bred a stubborn disposition among the men to hold him at all costs. Many times he felt the stinging lash of a doubled rope or the cut of a long whip as some cowboy raced alongside and dashed him back into the cattle under herd.

Experience had taught him that night was the best time to make a try for freedom. He learned to watch the night guard as they circled around in the darkness, and then to creep quietly away behind them. Once safely out of the herd, he would scurry away at full speed. But he learned, too, that a mere escape did not mean permanent liberty. Those keen-eyed range men had a habit of searching him out and invading his hiding-places, and routing him from them in a ruthless manner. He learned to keep close watch for any man on horseback, and to keep from sight as long as possible. Thus, the morning that the Old Hoss drove the last herd from the range Sancho stood upon a high point two miles away, watching with the alertness of a deer.

As soon as the Old Hoss was on his way, Dave Houston and another man swung around the range, bunching the cows and calves toward the center for the Old Hoss to inspect upon his return. Sancho had made his escape the last night without Dave's knowledge; therefore the cowboy was dumbfounded when he encountered him.

'Well, old outlaw,' Dave called out, 'you're slick when it comes to dodgin' around in the brush at night, but you ain't smart when it comes to pickin' out a range to winter on. You'll be sorry before this is over with. While them cattle out on the Pecos is wadin' around in grass knee-high, you'll be here starvin' to death on dead brush and oak leaves. When spring comes, about all that's liable to be left of you is a one-horned skeleton layin' around on some of these hills.'

When the Old Hoss returned, he and Dave made joint inspection of the mother cows and calves, and the Old Hoss voiced his alarm at their weakened condition.

'They'll never make it,' he said solemnly. 'If we don't get some stronger feed to help pull them along — half of them will never live to see spring.'

'They do look bad,' agreed Dave. 'But I don't know what can be done about it.'

'They say,' continued the Old Hoss, 'that these farmers are raising a good cow feed. It's the seed from cotton after the lint has been ginned away. If we can manage to get some, I think we'd better try it.'

'Yeah,' replied Dave with a skeptical tone in his voice, 'I've heard that too — but I never believed it. If that's so — it's the first time that a nester ever raised anythin' for a cowman but just plain hell. I always classed nesters about on par with sheep-herders.'

'Maybe so, maybe so,' the Old Hoss said with a smile. 'But there might be such a thing as reclassification. Wait until you get to scouting around through the settlements this winter buying feed, and see what another fine crop these nesters are raising.'

When Bill Sanders surmised that the range was being taken up in the east, his opinion was well founded. The vanguard of farmers was pushing out and settling over the range like rolling tumble weeds coming to rest in dry gulches. South and east of Coleman Town a colony of them had already formed and crowded out the large cow outfits. A thin string of scattering shacks led thirty miles south to where another settlement spread out on both sides of the Colorado.

Now, the Tree Top was in danger and the cowboys did not have to hunt very hard to find evidence of it. At the northeast corner of their range, where the Colorado looped itself into a magnificent horseshoe bend, a high bluff towered above the river. Upon a still day in the autumn a Tree Top cowboy could stop his horse upon this high bluff and hear the death knell of his trade being sounded in the soft purr of a cotton gin as the rows of spinning saws clipped lint cotton from the seed.

The Old Hoss went immediately to this gin and bought the entire lot of accumulated cottonseed. He started Dave Houston on a tour of all neighboring farms to buy up what surplus the farmers might have to sell. He set teamsters to freighting the purchased seed to the headquarters ranch, where they scooped them upon the ground and molded them into long ricks, while other men hauled out the daily feed allowance and scattered it to the starving cows and calves.

When the poor cows were first rounded up for feeding, Sancho's instinct told him that something was going on, but he kept himself aloof and viewed the activities from a safe distance. The scent of cottonseed carried a fragrant aroma to his dilating nostrils and he wondered if this pleasant scent did not have something good in store for him, and he decided to make further investigation.

While one man drove the team and the other pitched out the seed in huge scoopfuls, Sancho slid into the crowding cattle and breasted his way to the line of scattered seed. The smell was now delicious, and he could tell that the taste must be excellent too from the way other cattle struggled to get a bite; but his natural caution warned him to be careful. He was shy about picking up those fuzzy little balls and cramming them into his mouth. He smelled the seed and toyed with them between his lips and nibbled with uncertainty. But before his jaws had cracked a single hull, he was thrown into a panic at the bump of a horse's breast against his left side and the stinging lash of a doubled rope snapped along the full length of his back. He looked up in consternation and beheld the set face of his old enemy, Dave Houston.

'No, you don't, either!' challenged the cowboy as he spurred his horse after the retreating steer. 'You've missed yo'r chance at good feed this winter. Nary a bite of this cottonseed is goin' down yo'r throat or any other renegade steers that give us the dodge. It costs too much money,' he finished, taking another vicious swing with his rope at Sancho, who was now crashing into his sanctuary of brush.

True to Dave's words, Sancho and a few other getaway steers found themselves barred from every feed ground. He learned that when he put in appearance, it was only a signal for some cowboy to chase him away and whip him severely in the bargain. Many times during his flights to safety Dave's spinning loop rolled over his back and snaked out in the path of his plunging front feet and closed upon them. Then as Dave's horse whirled off at a tangent, Sancho would experience the sickening sensation of tumbling through space before crashing to the ground head first when his front feet were yanked high into the air and from under him. It did not require many instances of this rough treatment to break Sancho's spirit, and he finally gave up and moved out into the solitude of the range, where he devoted himself to the uphill task of securing food enough to keep life within his body.

Sancho found nothing on the open range to revive his spirit. The pickings were extremely lean, and, in spite of his rustling ability, he grew thin and snaky in flesh. His coat of glossy hair gradually transformed into a mat of shaggy wool; his hide lost its resilient stretch and drew tightly around his bony frame. His graceful stride devolved into a shambling reel, and his joints knocked together with each faltering step.

He searched up and down the rough hogbacks of the Brady Mountains for miles and ate every blade he could find of the dry and unpalatable grass in the foothills. He climbed laboriously to the mountain top and nipped at tough sotol stalks and live-oak brush on the summit. At the approach of a storm he would slither his way into the shelter of deep canyon gulches and stand in abject misery while cold rain or snow whipped over his shaking body — too weak and too despondent to seek warmth through exercise.

When mid-January came with its succession of sunny days, Sancho's spirit underwent a revival. He scoured hill and canyon with renewed energy and he was plunged into spasms of pain and sickness.

He had longed all winter for a taste of the prickly-pear cactus leaves which grew in such large clusters among the mesquite trees, but his numerous trials to get at them had always resulted in failure. He could never get his tongue or lips past the bristling array of pointed thorns which covered the leaves and were sharp enough to draw blood at the slightest touch.

He never ceased trying, however, and at last he discovered a single leaf of stunted growth with only a few scattering thorns protecting it. He licked around until he pulled a section of it into his mouth, and one taste of the juicy food set him wild. His hunger overcame caution, and he mouthed off large chunks of the thorny leaves and ground them into pulp and wolfed them down, heedless of the piercing thorns that were driving through sensitive tissues of his mouth lining.

That night he lay down upon a full stomach for the first time in months, but by morning a dull ache throbbed around his jawbones and in the roof of his mouth. Each hour through the following day found him in greater misery as the bearded thorns worked deeper and deeper into flesh and bone. Before night a reddish foam puffed from his lips and his swollen tongue forced its way between clinched teeth.

The maddening pain stifled his appetite. For a week Sancho lay in solitude and pain sheltered by his brush thicket, growing weaker as time sped on.

His inner being underwent a complete change, and he felt the natural urge of an animal to see the place of his birth before dying. He often turned his watery eyes toward the north, and bawled sadly as he contemplated the blue haze that hovered over the craggy hills outlining the Colorado's meandering course.

As the tide of strength ebbed lower, the pull took a stronger hold upon him and he rallied to obey the mandate of that call. He staggered painfully to his feet and in a blind trance wound his way down the head draws of a creek prong, and started his death march to the place of his birth upon the lower Mustang. Weakness encumbered his travel, and he was forced to make the journey in easy stages. He had great difficulty in crossing deep washouts along the way, and panted hard for breath after each exertion.

The exercise of walking loosened up stiff muscles and started his blood to flowing in a normal course. This tortured him with a bitter hunger. He also made a new discovery. He found that during the period of hibernation, Nature had worked for him one of her miraculous cures. The cactus spines that had tortured him so painfully were now dissolving into liquids and being washed away in his blood stream, and the soreness was leaving his mouth and tongue. At this time another pull took hold of him and he started rustling for food. Poor as the nourishment was, it lent him new energy and he pushed ahead When he reached the goal of his birthplace, he drove his steps on down the creek to halt amid the thick brush of the Colorado.

In the sheltered nooks of the river bottom, he found a few scattering sprigs of winter grass and weeds breaking through the ground crust. He gathered all of this scanty food within reach, but it was far from satisfying his appetite. His foraging carried him on down the river, and he crossed over the Tree Top boundary line at the northeastern corner of the range. Three miles farther on, he ran into a small bunch of farmer cattle that had come to the river for water. Sancho was almost as hungry for companionship as he was for food. These were the first cattle he had encountered since Dave Houston had hounded him so roughly.

Humbly he followed the little bunch of gentle cattle to their farm home, back on a tableland a mile from the river.

He shied with genuine alarm and walked with eyes and nose tense as he followed through the barn lot with its setting of corn cribs, harness shed, and granaries. He shook his head and stamped the ground in defiance at the smell of human beings and the hated canine scent which pervaded the premises. He was amazed at the careless way the gentle cattle disregarded these potent warnings. He trembled with hate and fear and was on the verge of flight, but his craving forced him to brave the dangers he felt so strongly.

He followed the cattle on through the barn lot onto a field of green winter oats. What a pleasant surprise was in store for him! Here was the best food he had ever tasted. One bite of that delicious oat forage made him cast all fears to the winds, and he gorged himself to the limit. He would remain upon this sweet feed and in the company of those ladylike milk cows the balance of his life. He did not know that already the farmer who owned the feed and the cows was looking upon him with disfavor.

He did not know that the farmer had no use for any cowman or their cows, and less use for the men that rode their horses. This particular farmer's only daughter had taken a fancy to Dave Houston when Dave paused long enough to buy feed during the winter. This had incensed the farmer's hostility to an extent that he despised the Tree Top worst of all. A few days after Sancho's arrival, Dave Houston paid a visit to the farmhouse and the steer came up for discussion.

'Yes, sir,' Dave agreed. 'I'll shore run 'im away, and if he comes back just let me know — I'll be right back after 'im.'

'Never mind about comin' back. If he don't stay away, I'll take care of 'im myself. I cain't figure out which I'd ruther have — a outlaw steer breakin' into my field or a cow waddie breakin' into my dinner table!'

Dave ran Sancho away that night, but he was careful to leave him close enough to insure his return. When the farmer stepped from his house next morning at daylight, he saw Sancho bogged to his belly in the heading oats.

'Damnation and tarnation and ever'thing else!' he shouted. 'If I don't drop that dad-blasted brute where he stands, it'll be 'cause I'm a pore shot.' He stormed into the house and unhung his long-barreled rifle from its rack of deer-horn pegs over the doorway.

'Now, Pa,' counseled the housewife, 'don't you go and do something rash that you'll repent for afterward. If you kill that steer, ever' hound of a cowboy in the country will be yappin' at us the balance of our lives. There's worse things can happen to us than feedin' outlaw steers and moochin' cowhands. You just content yerself with burnin' that brute with corn seed in the shotgun instead of shot.'

From the farmer's look as he strode toward the barn with his shotgun in the hollow of his arm, Sancho became alarmed. He had no fear of a man on foot, but this man was saddling a horse. He edged out of the danger zone, but moved too late. When he crashed through the fence a blistering charge of corn seed struck him broadside. The farmer hissed on his two vicious wolfhounds, and one of them fastened his teeth in Sancho's nose and swung with his full weight. Sancho flinched and the weight of the hound sprawled him to earth. Before he could recover, the other dog was upon him gnawing at his throat. By the time he shook them loose, another charge had been tamped into the shotgun, and he got it across his rump and back as he plunged away.

Whipping his horse into a gallop and yelling encouragement to his dogs, the farmer took out after Sancho. After three miles of panicky flight down the river, he abandoned the chase. Sancho's sides were heaving for breath and blood flowed from the gashes which marked him from nose to flank, and his body smarted where the corn seed had pelted him. He once more buried himself in the fastness of the brush to lick the soreness from his wounds.

For two days he lay still, and when hunger forced him from his hiding-place he decided to put himself further away from danger, and he sank deeper and deeper into the rough fastness of a new country. He traveled down the river until he came to the mouth of Saddle Creek, fifteen miles from the eastern border of his home range. Among the rough breaks in the river bottom he encountered twenty head of wild cattle of all ages and kinds. Some of the older ones wore brands, but most of them had never felt the sting of a hot iron.

At first they were suspicious of Sancho, and they sniffed angrily at the lingering dog scent upon him. But in time they accepted him as one of their own. To Sancho's surprise, he found that the winter grass had made a miraculous growth and that by diligent rustling he could get plenty of feed.

All during the month of March he remained in his new retreat undisturbed. He and his mates were ready to bolt away into the deep canyon gulches at the sight or smell of a human being, or they huddled together and formed a bank of horns and fighting heads at a threatened wolf attack. They waded or splashed across the Colorado at will and worked up and down both sides of the stream.

At first, Sancho's timidity of running water caused him much uneasiness, but as he followed his mates back and forth his old fear was overcome and he found much joy in breasting the strong current. He learned that he could swim with the same ease and certainty that he walked and ran. His immense lung capacity especially adapted him for a swimmer. His deep breath intakes swelled his sides back to his hips, and the confined air kept his body afloat with little effort. The strength of his strong legs and the willowy twist of his body drove him through the water with remarkable speed. It was only a short time until the former water-shy steer was leading, instead of following the bunch of cattle as they crossed and recrossed the stream, giving little heed to high or low stages of the water.

CHAPTER NINE
SANCHO MEETS BEN HARTE

O N TOP of the Brady Mountain fifteen miles east of the Tree Top boundary line, twenty miles south of the Colorado, and twice the distance south of Coleman Town, a trail outfit was breaking camp and getting under way. The cook was busy stowing away his utensils; two men were harnessing the six-mule team while two others loaded beds and camp equipment into the wagon. The wrangler was coiling the ropes of his corral, and a *remuda* of a hundred horses, showing strong evidence of their Arabian blood grazed slowly away from camp. The horses were branded the deuce of hearts — a small figure upon each left shoulder and thigh.

A little man with a pointed red beard sat cross-legged upon the ground, sipping coffee and staring into the dying fire. Clamped against the ground by the heel of his boot was the tip end of a bridle rein, holding a snuff-colored brown horse which tossed his head and rolled a pair of flashing eyes. The Mexican cook picked up the blackened coffee-pot and approached the sitting man.

'*Quieres mas café*, Señor Harte-Corazon?' he asked, standing respectfully at the small man's side.

Ben Harte ignored the other's words. Then, without comment, he dumped the remaining coffee and grounds into the bed of smoldering coals and handed the empty cup to the waiting cook. He pulled the bridle rein free and stood up.

'A hell of a country,' he muttered. He gave the horse a vicious kick in the side and his voice trailed off into a deeper oath. 'Not enough grass on a thousand acres to keep a crow alive.'

The cook swept the team around in a wide circle and started down the trail. Harte stepped gingerly into his stirrup and swung upon his horse. He rode out to where a bearded, dirty-faced man was bellowing orders to a mixed crew of white and Mexican cowboys. They were pointing the lead cattle of a large herd of long-horned steers toward a gap in the Brady Mountains. The cattle were branded with a large heart upon the left side. From where Harte stood looking at the gap it resembled the tree of a huge saddle dished out of the mountain top. The deep gashes led into twisting gully washes at the foot, which then straightened out and broke away into the main prong of Saddle Creek.

Harte had good reason for his dissatisfaction with range conditions. After leaving the breaks of the Llanos he had entered the drouth area of the previous year and encountered bad going. This country was the worst of the entire strip. It was known as 'no man's land.' Bleak desolation told of the hundreds of loose horses and thousands of drifting sheep that had wintered there.

Harte had voiced his determination to cross the Colorado before nightfall. He knew that cowmen north of the river had waged a determined warfare upon the poaching horses and sheep, and that better grass awaited his cattle there. He had given strict orders to his major-domo, Jack Barnes, to push the herd to the limit of the animals' endurance.

Added to his other worries was the reported condition of the river. He had learned that the flow of water lately had been alternating between the fording and flooded stage. The heavy rain-clouds hanging over the upper reaches of the stream for the last two nights held little promise of an easy crossing, and there was a threat of holding him up indefinitely.

A look of cruel determination lurked in his shifting eyes as he rode to one side and watched his men urging the string of three thousand gaunt and hungry steers down the long slopes at a rapid walk in their forced drive to the river. Guttural oaths rolled from his throat when he looked far away at the line of green trees which marked the watercourse.

'A hell of a river,' he muttered. 'Not enough water to float a goose in for nine months of the year, but too much to cross a wagon in the other three. I'd like to see the whole country in hell.'

A lean-faced Mexican whose feet dangled from long legs near his horse's knees rode by in his proper place with the herd, and Harte beckoned to him.

'Juan,' Harte rasped, looking at the stolid brown face with overhanging eyebrows and dropping mouth corners, 'we gottee too much water in reev-er. She rain too much in high country up yonder' — with a wide sweep of his hand toward the northwest. 'Mebbe so she come down in too much beeg rise today.'

The scowl upon the Mexican's face softened. '*Si, señor,*' he smiled. '*Me sabe bien.* Reev-er she too bad — *muy malo.* Go like-a thees,' he continued, throwing his hands in a rolling motion.

'Shut up!' stormed Harte. 'Wait till you're told to speak!'

'*Si, señor,*' acquiesced the Mexican, lapsing into silence.

'I don't want none of yo'r lip,' continued Harte. 'But what I want is for you to go help that wrangler and cook and git that wagon across.'

The scowl settled upon the Mexican's face again.

'Mebbe so — wagon, mules — go wash down reev-er and go drown,' he said, showing the alarm of a hill man at the thought of deep and running water.

'You'd better not let them mules drown,' growled Harte. 'If you do, you'd better drown yo'rself — or I'll make you wish you had.'

Harte's fingers tightened around the handle of his quirt. 'I want that there wagon across before the river gits too high. Sabe?

We can swim the cattle and hosses — but not the wagon. Now git out, before I give you a taste of this quirt.'

All forenoon the cattle hurried toward the river, and Harte swore. He punished his own horse, cursed at his men and threatened their lives. When Juan returned to the herd five miles back from the river and proudly informed him that the wagon was safely across, Harte spoke his first civil words of the day.

'Que tan hondo esta el rio ahora?' asked Harte.

'Esta desta hondo,' answered Juan; as if measuring the depth, he swept his open palm along the bottom of his saddle skirt. 'Yo creo estará deste hondo cuanda llegamos aya con el ganado,' he added. Dropping his bridle reins over the fork of his saddle and leaning forward, he now flopped his arms in a swimming motion.

'All right,' replied Harte. 'I don't give a damn if she's deep enough to swim a ship, just so that wagon's across. You've done all right for a chuckle-headed Mexican — so for that you can stay up here with me and we'll help the point drivers push the lead cattle into the reev-er.'

When the thirsty cattle caught the smell of river water and the lead animals quickened their stride, it was only a short time until they were dropping down into the thorny brush at the mouth of Saddle Creek. While Harte and the Mexican Juan rode slightly ahead, holding the plunging lead cattle in line and letting them down through the brush in a skillful manner, they ran squarely onto Sancho and his wild mates where they lay sunning in an open glade. At the tramp of the herd coming down upon them the dozing animals dashed away.

'Git them cattle! Git them cattle!' Harte yelled, spurring his own horse after the fleeing bunch. 'Them's a bunch of real water dogs. They ain't afeared of water. They'll make good leaders to put in front of my dogies and coax 'em into the river.'

Sancho bored into the thick brush, followed by his slower mates. He glanced backward and saw a cow pony, with fiery eyes and ears laid back, crowding close upon him. He came to an abrupt stop and whirled away from the crowding horse. The cow pony's legs bent under like a flexed spring, and his lithe body swept around from the recoil in such a low turn that Juan's boot-heel jabbed upon the ground. The horse rushed him and thrust his head forward; his foaming mouth opened, and two rows of gleaming teeth closed upon a pinch of hide on Sancho's shoulder.

The steer whirled, and Harte drove his horse to the opposite side from Juan and they closed down at the same time. Sancho found himself between two vicious horses, bearing two determined men who struck him cutting raps with their long quirts. His mates were standing in a frightened huddle under guard of the two point drivers, and the only course open to Sancho was to rejoin them. As he did so, the lead cattle of Harte's trail herd broke into the little clearing. The point drivers dropped back to their stations; Harte and Juan separated and swung slightly to one side, and Sancho found himself leading the way toward the river.

He broke into a swinging gallop, and hurried forward with his mates crowding close upon his heels. The Harte cowboys were now driving hard against the lead cattle, bringing them along at a brisk trot. Sancho paused at the rolling water heaving under its burden of red silt from far back in the high country, where it was stirred up and washed away from the Red Beds which served as underpinning for the Staked Plains.

The howling, quirt-wielding horsemen and the crowding trail cattle hurried him into the water. He thrust his nose high, and with a deep breath filled his lungs to their full capacity. His sides swelled and his body lay awash like a drifting log. He leveled off, and the drive of his long legs shoved him toward the north shore. When he looked back the river was full of cattle, bending down stream before the current like a huge U. The string broke, and those on the south bank refused to enter. Harte and

Juan cut Sancho and his mates out and swam them back to the awed cattle, and used them again as leaders.

Three times they were crossed back and forth before their work was done and the last of the trail cattle struggled up the north bank at sundown. Sancho became lost from his mates, but nevertheless he spent a pleasant night, visiting and rubbing horns with his newly-found acquaintances from faraway southern Texas. And around the campfire, Harte's men were singing his praise as a leader.

While getting his herd started next morning, Harte instructed his foreman, Jack Barnes, to hold everything they had picked up the night before except she cattle.

'I think we'd better cut that there one-horned steer,' Barnes protested. 'I couldn't make out his brand last night, but from his earmark I'd say he's a Tree Top. It's a hard outfit to work on. They've got cowhands scattered ever'where, and the brand is knowed wherever cattle are run. It's just about as hard to get away with a Tree Top steer as it is to hide a barrel of water under yo'r coat-tail.'

'Do like I tell you,' snarled Harte. 'I'm boss today and I'm dishin' out the powders.'

'All right,' muttered the foreman. 'You're the doctor.'

'Yes, I'm the doctor,' Harte growled. 'That Ol' Hoss Denman has got his whizzer run on a lot of fellers, but not on me. I've heered tell how he's always a-blowin' about what good men he's got. If some of them fancy cowhands of his'n comes nosin' around, I'll show what good men and good shots they is with this outfit too.'

At this time Sancho walked by, and both men stared at his branded side. Harte batted his eyes and wondered if they were playing him tricks. He turned Sancho so the sunlight fell squarely against his brand. Then he threw back his head and cackled in derision at Barnes.

'You try to tell me to leave that steer?' he shouted. And before his companion could speak, he answered his own question. 'Not by a damned sight. I ain't never been accused of leavin' a ox in my own brand and I ain't goin' to start now. That steer has got mighty nigh as purty a heart on 'im as you could draw with paper and pencil.'

No, Harte decided, his eyes had not played him a trick. The muddy water of the Colorado had worked the deception. The day before a mat of hair had covered the brand on Sancho's side. Now, the dropping limbs of the Tree Top stood out while the stem of the tree lay buried under a layer of long hair and settlings from the muddy water. Both outside tips of the Tree Top limbs supported a ridge of hair roached up by the lapping current as it swished around the swimming steer's side. These two ridges came together four inches below and formed an open V. The combination made a presentable heart.

'But that won't stay,' objected Barnes.

'The hell it won't!' stormed Harte. 'Them ridges is stuck tight with mud that's about as tough as paste. They'll stay there till we swim another river anyhow, and that'll be long after we've got out of Tree Top territory.'

CHAPTER TEN
BEN HARTE'S HERD
IS CUT

COLEMAN TOWN lies snuggled against the foot of a north-and-south hill range that stretches in a broken chain from the Brazos to the Colorado. A rolling plain drops gently away from the eastern base. Cattle trails from the vast country between the Colorado and Rio Grande struggled out of the deep brush and merged together at the southern tip of the open plain.

It had long been a joking comment that a successful trail man was one who could keep his number good. This meant that he would contrive to reach his destination with as many cattle or more than he had started with, and in this way cover his actual losses sustained during the trip. But many unscrupulous trail men discarded the joke element and acted with all seriousness. Because of this practice, wayside cattlemen along the trail lost heavily from depredations of thieves.

In time, steps were taken to correct the situation, and cowmen in the territory surrounding Coleman Town banded themselves into an association. They planned to place good brand men as inspectors at a point where the trails came together to cut out strayed cattle from the passing herds.

The Old Hoss was a leader in the association, and it was only natural that he should have a voice in selecting the inspectors. He knew that there was no better brand man in the country than

Bill Sanders; therefore, it was only logical that Bill should receive the appointment.

All the Tree Top steers that had wintered on the Pecos were sold to resident cowmen, and there was no herd to drive to market. The others were returned to the ranch, and the Tree Top men simply marked time and waited. For reasons which he kept to himself, Bill Sanders was highly elated to learn that his duties required him to move into a camp near Coleman Town. The first of April found him installed with an assistant and vested with legal authority to hold and inspect moving herds and to cut out any animal belonging to the membership of the association.

It had been a busy day for Bill Sanders and his assistant, Matt Cook. They had recovered nearly a hundred head of cattle that would have been lost to their owners had it not been for the inspection. They made a throwback of these animals down on the Red Bank Creek, south of Coleman Town, and were returning to their camp at dusk. On their way, they discovered a large herd of long-horned cattle being rounded into shape upon a bed ground. Four men rode by in front of the inspectors at a quartering angle toward the herd. They wore high crowned hats of the Mexican style and plain leather chaps, and bull-winged *tapaderos* flopped loosely from stirrups. The sharpeared, bulging-eyed horses which the men rode held Bill's interest. He strained his eyes trying to locate a brand on them.

'Looks like a South Texas outfit,' commented Matt. 'Them boys are all dressed up for brush and cactus ridin'.'

The inspectors topped the rise and saw the camp ahead. Bed rolls were scattered in confused array around the chuck wagon. A dozen or fifteen horses stood saddled on stake. Several men lounged around the fire. A white sheet sagged across the wagon bows. The dark lines of a heart drawn with wagon tar upon the sheet stood out against the bleached canvas.

'Yo'r guess ain't far from right,' agreed Bill, letting his eye run hurriedly over the men, the wagon, and their horses. 'But

I can go you one better and guess the outfit's name. We'll stop and introduce ourselves. I've heard this outfit is kind of salty, but we'd just as well git acquainted and start the ball to rollin'.'

Bill saw a small middle-aged man sitting cross-legged in front of the fire. A pair of high-heeled boots with saddle-worn tops encased a pair of feet small enough for a woman. The crown of his hat came to a six-inch point, and the wide brim pulled low enough to almost hide a pair of shifting beady eyes. A hawklike nose curved over and lost itself in a heavy red mustache. A Van Dyked beard pointed toward his open shirt front.

Upon his right sat a murky-faced, unshaven man of heavier than medium weight and build. In his hand was a small stick with which he sat marking lines in the dirt at his feet. Across the fire from the two men were ranged a dozen others, about evenly divided between Mexicans and white men. One in particular held Bill's attention. He was a long, lean-bodied Mexican. Eyebrows as dark as crow's feathers drooped over a pair of flashing eyes that resembled the sparks of fire popped from the burning wood. His left side leaned against a bed roll. His long legs stretched out in front, the toes of his rough boots stuck straight up, and the large spoke rowels of his silver-mounted spurs dug into the ground. Sideways to the firelight he held in his hands a half-completed riding quirt — the handle was gamboled from the stub of a mesquite bush. In the flickering light Bill could see the Mexican's fingers darting in and out of the maze of rawhide strings like the beaks of carnivorous fowls pecking at shreds of meat.

'Who's the boss?' asked Bill as he dismounted.

The hum of slurring Spanish words came to a sudden hush at the sound of Bill's voice. A puzzled frown spread itself under the small man's hatbrim. He twisted his neck around until he could peep sideways at the inspector's horses where he appeared to study their brands in the dim firelight. His right hand reached toward a side vest pocket and his fingers jerked out a sack of tobacco, while his left hand secured a slip of brown paper from another pocket. He creased the paper and spilled a few grains of tobacco in it. While the sack was being returned, the fingers of his left hand magically twisted paper and tobacco into a cigarette. His right hand came out from the pocket and brought a match which burst into flame on its way. He sucked deep drafts from the freshly lighted cigarette, and heavy clouds of smoke shot from both nostrils.

'Guess I c'd be called the boss,' he said, taking a step forward and scowling at Bill's horse. 'Bein's I own the outfit, guess I can tend to business. My name's Harte.'

'Mine's Sanders,' Bill replied, offering his hand, which was ignored.

'I see by the brand on yer hosses that you're a Tree Top man,' Harte resumed. 'Now, I wonder whut business some of Ol' Hoss Denman's men've got with this outfit.'

'We ain't exactly Tree Top men any more,' Bill offered by way of explanation. 'You might say we're a-ridin' borrowed hosses. Me and my pardner here work for a lot of different outfits. We're brand inspectors.'

'You're whut?' asked Harte, rolling his eyes in an apparent attempt to appear amazed. 'What's them things you're a-talkin' about got to do with me?'

Bill slipped a match stick from the end of his cigarette. 'I said we're brand inspectors,' he repeated slowly. 'It's our business to watch trail herds and see that they don't drive off any cattle belonging to members of the Association. I aim to cut yo'r herd tomorrow. You savvy what that means, don't you?'

A wave of crimson edged its way along Harte's cheeks and his eyes flashed a cold glitter. 'Yeah. I know what you mean all right,' he replied, 'but that don't mean nothin' to me. I ain't got no cattle but what's mine, and if you think I'll hold up these dogies while some pompadour cowhand slashes around among 'em to drag out ever'thing that ain't got my heart on 'em — why, you've got another guess a-comin'.'

'I've got a little book,' said Bill, tapping his vest pocket. 'This book has got a list of brands that belong to the Association. I'll cut you tomorrow for these brands——'

'And I say you cain't do it, mister insect, or whatever you call yerself,' Harte retorted in a high-pitched voice, his beady eyes slanted down to a point.

The hush of the camp deepened and there was a slight shifting of positions. Bill shot a quick glance around and found Matt standing at ease with his left hand dangling at his side. His right thumb was sticking into his belt a few inches back of his gun handle. The man who had been sitting next to Harte had arisen and substituted the small stick for a spade. He stood jabbing the edge of it lightly into the ground. The lanky Mexican paused in his quirt-making and let the parts of it swing free from the stub bush. He squared around to where he looked directly over the fire at the four men. He had pushed himself back against the bed roll, and his long legs were now folded under him as he sat like a rattlesnake ready to strike.

'All set and ready to go,' murmured Bill. Just as he was ready to step forward and crash his fist into Harte's leering mouth, he heard the echo of a soft-spoken voice at his ear droning an admonition.

'Remember, Bill,' the Old Hoss had said when the sheriff pinned the badge of a deputy upon his vest lapel. 'You're an officer of the law now, and you'll have to lay personal feelings aside. We don't want to have any killing scrapes. If we'd wanted a man that would fly off the handle at the first personal insult, we'd have given the job to Dave Houston. We want a man that can read brands, that's not afraid to call a bluff, and that keeps a cool head at all times.'

Bill stepped back, a thin smile on his flushed face. 'All right, you've had yo'r say. I'll have mine tomorrow. I'll hold this herd up and go through it like a fine-toothed comb goes through the head of a lousy Indian.'

'And don't forget, mister insector, I'll be at the combin',' Harte flung after them as Bill and Matt turned their horses and rode away.

After the inspectors had departed, a buzz conversation of mixed Spanish and English arose from the other side of the fire. But Harte had little thought for the conversation of his men. He rolled another cigarette with shaking fingers. The pallor of cold fury lay set around his tightly drawn features.

'I'll show a couple of smart alecs about whose runnin' this here outfit — even if I have to kill 'em——'

'But Ben,' spoke up his cautious lieutenant. 'Don't you know we cain't buck open-handed agin the law?'

'To hell and damnation with the law,' Harte exploded. 'Ain't they more of us than they is of them?'

'But Ben,' the other persisted. 'We're in the other feller's country now. That there cowhand is got us foul. He's got the star of the law, and the law can git a hundred men if it needs 'em. He can git a bunch of them Rangers to help. You ain't forgot whut they done to us oncest, have you? Don't you think they're trigger fingers is jes' itchin' to do it again?'

Harte resumed his seat without replying. During the night, however, he mulled over the counsel of his man and admitted to himself that he had made a mistake in trying to bluff the inspector. He knew that if he refused to permit him to cut his herd next day, there would be trouble. He swore deeply and wickedly, but long before he went to sleep that night he made up his mind that the wisest way out was to let the inspector cut his herd.

His decision was influenced further next morning when three horsemen appeared at his herd along with the two inspectors. They were strangers to Harte, but they looked familiar. He had seen their kind before, to his own sorrow. They carried short-barreled Winchesters swung underneath their right legs. A heavy pistol hung from their belts on each side. An extra bandolier of ammunition lay across their saddle forks. All this identified them clearly as Texas Rangers.

Harte rode across the lead of his walking herd to where his major-domo was driving the other point. 'We're whupped,' he said with a savage oath. 'The cyards is stacked agin me, and their ain't no use'n buckin' a loosin' game. Damn the whole country anyhow,' he growled. 'I wish it and ever'body in it was in hell.'

'Ben,' continued Barnes with hesitation, 'you'd better git yerself ready to cut loose from that there one-horned steer. I'd bet my spurs that that boss inspector has already got 'im spotted by the earmark.'

'Earmark and be damned!' Harte snarled again. 'Are you afeared of somethin'? You know them earmarks don't mean nothin'. All them Valderman cattle we're drivin' is marked swallow fork on the left — jus' like this one-horned steer. Why couldn't he belong to them cattle jes' as well as the Tree Top?'

'He could all right,' Barnes agreed sourly. 'But he ain't — and I'll bet that there inspector knows he ain't.'

'Whut's gittin' into you?' Harte barked again. 'If you're afeared, you'd better cut yer string of hosses and git out while yer hide's whole. I'm a-goin' to hold on to that there one-horned steer or fight ever' damned pistol-tottin' officer in these parts. Them there inspector waddies'll never know the difference. Jus' watch me.' With those last words Harte rode around to where Bill Sanders and one of the Rangers were engaged in conversation.

'The herd's yo'rs any time you want it,' he said with a seductive tone in his voice and an imitation of a pleasant smile. 'Jes' have a leetle mercy on a feller and don't cut me too close.'

Bill made no reply, but when the herd arrived upon an open flat, just one mile south of Coleman Town, he ordered it held up and he and Matt went to work.

While searching through the herd, Bill's eyes had come to rest upon Sancho many times, and he puzzled over the brand on the steer's side. 'That's my little pet steer,' he muttered confidently to Matt Cook, 'but there's something that's kind of spooky about 'im, and I've got to find out about it. For instance,' resumed Bill, 'how did Harte ever git his hands on 'im? If he made that Tree Top over into a heart, when did he do it? I saw that steer last fall, and a made-over brand ain't had time to cure up like that one is since then.'

'Maybe that there Mexican bronc-twister that Bob had there last fall burnt the brand into a heart,' Matt suggested.

'Not hardly,' replied Bill. 'He didn't have a chance to. Then if he did, what became of that tree stem? A feller can work a brand over all right, but he cain't rub part of it out.'

'Then maybe you're wrong,' answered Matt. 'There's lots of earmarks the same. Maybe this ain't the steer you think he is.'

'Don't let that git into yo'r head,' scoffed Bill. 'I'd know that steer's hide in a tan yard. I know 'im for a hundred different reasons — the most important of 'em are: I put that earmark on 'im myself and I know how it was made. I know the cut of white on his face and around his eyes. I know 'im from the way he travels. I know 'im by the way he keeps his eye pasted on us all the time. It's him all right, but let's see what Harte has to say.'

'Don't you know when to quit?' asked Harte, as Bill rode up to him and he again assumed his pleasant front.

'Just about done now,' grunted Bill. 'But there's one I ain't sure of——' Swinging around in his saddle he pointed to Sancho. 'Where did you get that steer?'

'Whut steer you talkin' about?' Harte asked.

'I mean that one-horned steer there at the edge of the herd.'

'Oh, that steer,' answered Harte. 'I bought 'im down on the Guadalupe frum a old Dutchman.'

Bill motioned to one of the Rangers, who responded by riding up to them.

Bill continued, 'What's the name of that man you bought the steer from?'

'His name's Valderman,' Harte said hesitatingly, eyeing the Ranger. 'I bought about a hundred head. They's all branded VM but this one.'

'Ah, I see,' acquiesced Bill. 'Then if you know all about 'im not bein' branded, you probably know how come his horn's off.'

'Shore,' responded Harte with an easy breath and cunning grin. 'I know all about that too. As I says, he's the only one not branded. When we drove the bunch home and jes' afore we turned 'em loose, one of the boys roped this ox so's we could brand 'im and he piled up too hard and broke a horn. It was cracked so bad that I jes' finished the job by whackin' it off smooth with my knife.'

'Shore,' Bill agreed quietly. 'I might've knowed it would be somethin' like that. But it's real funny about how many horns some steers will grow. He's got a good one that's never been touched. You say you cut one off, and I know I cut one off myself.'

The grin on Bill's face had faded, and he turned to face Harte.

'What you got to say about that?' he asked. 'Do you want to give that steer up without any argument, or will I have to go through the rigamarole of ropin', throwin', and shearin' off the hair on his side to prove that there's a Tree Top brand under that ball of long hair and river mud?'

Harte's assumed pleasantness departed. A look of sullen rage was spreading over his countenance while Bill talked.

'I ain't goin' to give up nothin',' he rasped.

'Just as you say,' continued Bill pleasantly. 'If you make me prove this steer, I'll do it, but I'll stretch my distance and go a little farther. I'll swear out a warrant and have you arrested for stealing cattle and make you prove to a court and jury's satisfaction how you come by this one steer and all them other stray cattle we've cut from yo'r herd today. When a feller claims to know all about a steer — flesh marks and all — and that he cut a horn off that he didn't — that's too much. And I've got a witness right here to prove ever' word you said about it too.'

Harte's eyes shifted back and forth from Bill to the Ranger. His face reddened and then turned ashen pale. He pulled up tight on his bridle reins; his right hand slid around his right side and came to rest near the butt of his gun. He swallowed — then looked again at the Ranger.

'Take that damn steer and go to hell with him!' Harte almost screamed at Bill Sanders. 'I'd be in a fine kettle of soapgrease if I ever got into court in this country. I don't settle my rows that way nohow. I settle at the point of a gun, and that's where I'll settle with you some time too.'

As Harte continued to talk, his voice rose to a higher pitch and his fury seemed to increase beyond control. 'It ain't nothin' but a trumped-up deal agin me,' he yelled. 'You call yerselfs officers. You act more like a gang of robbers.'

Suddenly he drove the sharp rowels of his spurs into his horse's side. The animal flinched, reared straight up, and struck hard with its forefeet in protest against the brutal assault.

'Git goin', there,' Harte called to his men. 'Git this herd on the move before I bust loose and cut a damned inspector's heart right outen his breast.'

Bill Sanders signaled Matt Cook to cut Sancho and throw him with the other recovered cattle. The rangy steer dashed away with Matt hot after him, and Bill turned his attention again to the enraged rustler.

'So long, Ben,' he called. 'You'd better cool off and forget it. Be a little careful from now on about how you try to pull a one-horned steer. You might git somebody else's pet. I know this little ox better than you know yo'r own horse. Me and him is *puros compañeros*.'

Bill drove the cattle he recovered from Harte back to the Red Bank and turned them loose among the farm settlements. Sancho liked the association of gentle cows, but at this time of year, he found each one of these little bunches ruled by a herd bull. These bulls hooked and abused him unmercifully until he learned a trick that allowed him to stampede the surliest of the lot. When he locked horns with them in combat he learned that the absence of his left horn would permit him to make a quick slip of his head to one side. He would then drive the point of his right horn deep into his adversary's neck or shoulder and stampede him in a wild panic. In time he went his way unchallenged and he ruled the whole domain.

He developed into a night prowler, and made a nuisance of himself to any trail herd that stopped overnight in the vicinity. He would bore his way into the herd under cover of darkness and maintain a disturbance the balance of the night by routing any animal that had the courage to stand before him in battle. He became a familiar figure to all trail men, and he was advertised from the Flint Hills of Kansas to the Rio Grande.

Harte moved the herd on to Kansas and experienced a decided run of bad luck. While driving across the Indian Territory he was beset by a number of stampedes and lost cattle in all of them. He assumed that Indians had caused the stampedes and made away with the lost animals under cover of darkness. When he reached his destination he sold his herd upon a low market and, in a fit of despondency he sold his *remuda* of saddle horses, reserving only a light team and a horse for himself and his foreman. He set his men adrift owing them most of their year's wages and, facing a financial crisis, he and his foreman, Barnes, and the Mexican, Juan, hurried back over the trail to Texas. They arrived in Coleman Town upon a late day in October in the midst of a cold, drenching rain. After camping for the night, Harte voiced his determination to replace all his losses by stealing other cattle and moving them to his ranch in the breaks of the Nueces.

CHAPTER ELEVEN

'THAT ONE-HORNED STEER IS PIZEN'

Next morning the weather had cleared. To any casual inquirer, Harte intimated that he was waiting for the roads to settle, but he had another reason. He knew that many unbranded young cattle belonging to farmers were ahead of him. He knew that one night's drive would put him safely in the rough breaks of the Colorado.

The three travelers broke camp in the evening and drove out through town, stopping only long enough to add a few provisions to their supply. Harte and Barnes rode ahead of Juan, who drove a spring wagon. They pushed on to Red Bank Creek and made another stop. The wagon was not unloaded, and only the bridle bits were slipped from their horses' mouths. While the men squatted around a small campfire and ate a light supper, Harte was moved to enthusiasm.

'Look, boys! Look!' he exclaimed when a small bunch of cattle passed close to their camp. 'Look at them unbranded yearlin's and two-year-old cattle. Here's where we start to work.'

He gave brusque orders and outlined his plans for the night. He ordered Juan to strip the harness from one of the work horses and place his saddle upon him. When Juan was mounted, the three of them rode away and started a small round-up drive. Within an hour they were back together again, holding a hundred head of farmer cattle. Harte broke into a spasm of gaiety when he recognized Sancho among them.

Thirty minutes of wild riding in the gathering dusk followed while the riders cut out the young and unbranded animals. With Sancho among them, they drove the bunch at a terrific gait for two miles. 'Give it to 'em, boys,' Harte ordered, plying his quirt with brutal cruelty.

When they at last permitted the winded animals to slow up and catch their breath, Harte sent Juan back for the wagon. He then ordered Juan to drive down the regular traveled road to a point near the Colorado River twenty miles away, and there turn a mile downstream and make camp. Harte and Barnes now drove the little bunch of stolen cattle on a near cut through the hills and brush.

'But Ben,' objected the cautious Barnes after the flurried cattle settled down to a calm walk and gave the two men a chance for conversation. 'That onehorned steer is pizen to us. He's a regular Jonah. We cain't never git away with him. That Tree Top brand is too hard to work over. Besides, he's been looked at too many times. He's knowed from the no'th pint of Kansas to the southe'n tip of Texas. There's not a cow waddie this side of the Smoky River that don't know 'im by flesh marks alone.'

'Don't git the trembles agin,' grunted Harte. 'I ain't afeared to match thumbs with them Tree Top waddies. When we git that steer home, I'll make that brand look like the Spanish rosette. I'll rub out some of them noted flesh marks of his'n too.'

'You cain't rub out nature's marks,' argued Barnes.

'Cain't I?' questioned Harte scornfully. 'You jus' wait. I'll show yuh a trick or two. I'll saw off that one horn down deep into his head. I'll slice off the other side to match and make 'im look like a natural muley when he gits well. Then I'll bob off about six j'ints of his tail and grub them ears down into his neck. I'll break up his gait by takin' out a inch of the main leader in a hind leg. That'll make 'im limp a little, travel sort of slanchwise, and drag a foot when he gits in a hurry. When that's all done and we've wintered 'im at home, I'll drive 'im back under their noses next spring.'

'Yep, that's all humpty-dumpty,' replied Barnes. 'But you mightn't git a chancest to do all that. Them inspectors is liable to be barkin' at our tracks inside of twenty-four hours. I tell you that there steer is bad medicine and he means *malo suerte* for us.'

'I jus' hope he does. I jus' hope he does start on our trail,' Harte mused, unmindful of Barnes's finishing words.

After getting his wind back, Sancho, at the first chance, edged into a rocky canyon. When he turned into the brush, he heard the swish and crack of tree limbs as a man's body crashed among them. Instantly, a horse and rider reached his side and he heard a deep-throated oath and felt the stinging cut of a quirt tail across his back. He gave way before the furious pressure, and swung around in a half circle. He soon found himself back in the midst of the little bunch of cattle.

He now angled through the fast-traveling cattle and tried a different ruse. This time he dashed boldly across a strip of open ground, and depended upon the advantage of his start and speed to carry him beyond danger. Again the attempt ended in failure. A snuff-colored brown horse, bearing a small man with a flaming red beard, bore down upon him. Again he felt the cruel lashes of a whip and he was forced back.

All night long, the cattle were rushed through rough canyons and over rocky hillsides until they were ready to drop from exhaustion. At last they found better going when they were turned down a wide draw which led into the Colorado bottoms. As the morning sunlight played across the rugged breaks of the river, they were brought to a stop in a small opening, hedged about by tall trees and heavy growths of underbrush. The camp wagon stood at the far edge of the clearing. The two work horses were chewing at the tough growth of bottom grass. The Mexican

Juan stood over a blazing fire surrounded by pots and pans of steaming food. The tired cattle dropped to the ground.

All day long they rested in this hidden spot. Late in the day while returning from a hunt, the camp was discovered by a fifteen-year-old boy who lived in the Red Bank settlement. Behind a screen of brush, he watched an armed man who appeared to be guarding the cattle. He noticed two other men lying in bed at the camp.

While the boy watched, Sancho raised his head and scrambled to his haunches. The boy recognized Sancho immediately, for he had run the outlaw from his father's field many times. Closer inspection showed him other cattle belonging to his farmer neighbors. He was now positive that these animals were being stolen. He backed his saddle horse out of sight and as quickly as he could rode the twenty miles to Coleman Town and told Bill Sanders what he had seen.

Traveling light, Bill Sanders and Matt Cook left town at midnight. They wished to be on the ground at daylight in order to pick up the trail.

It was an easy matter to locate the abandoned camp and find evidence to bear out the boy's story. They followed cattle tracks and wheel marks of a light rig winding across the river to high ground beyond. Here, baffling circumstances arose to meet them. The wagon tracks swung to the southwest and the cattle tracks turned sharply back to the north and melted away.

'Why not follow the wagon?' asked Matt while Bill examined the ground.

'That's what a smart cow thief would want us to do,' replied Bill. 'In that way he'd have a double lookout. The wagon driver could spot us and fire a gun, build a smoke signal, or do 'most any number of things to warn the fellers with the cattle that they're being followed and give 'em a chance to cut loose. We want to find them cattle with the thieves drivin' them.'

Bill dismounted when he glimpsed a dim imprint of a shod horse's foot in a bare spot of ground. He then followed the horse's tracks back to the river sand along with a few cow tracks.

'They've crossed back to the north side,' Bill commented.

'But there ain't no trail,' objected Matt. 'There's just a scatterin' track now and then like range cattle make when they come and go to water.'

'That's where the fancy work of a good cow thief comes in,' Bill replied. 'He's scattered them cattle so's they won't leave a trail—just like the Injuns done a long time ago when they raided through the country. This feller knew his business, but if we look close enough we'll find tracks bunched together somewhere north of the river and on high ground.'

Bill looked across to the high hills on the north side. He then turned and scanned the rolling country to the southwest where he could make out distant landmarks in the Tree Top range. He looked again at the direction the wagon tracks were taking and he shook his head.

'We're up agin a first-class thief all right,' he mused, 'but I'm ready to make a guess with 'im. I'll bet my head that a gent by the name of Ben Harte is directin' this show, and them cattle with Sancho among 'em is steppin' off the distance toward his hangout on the Nueces.'

Bill knew of an ideal hiding-place twenty-five miles down the river. He turned to his partner.

'I'm goin' to make another guess,' he said. 'When them cattle left here, they headed straight for the Devil's Hole. They're in there right now restin'. We'll never overtake 'em if we stick to a trail. They'll probably break camp about sundown and move on. We'd better hit our leather and ride straight to the Hole before they git started.'

While the sun hung two hours above the western horizon, the inspectors paused on the brink of a disrupted and scarred sink of landscape. From their position they commanded a sweep of the entire countryside. Three miles south of the river, a thin column of smoke puffed out and spiraled upward. The column broke and faded away; then it reappeared and vanished — and reappeared again.

'It's all over but the shoutin' now,' Bill complained. 'I'll bet money or marbles that the wagon driver has passed word on to his pardners that they're bein' followed, and wherever them cattle are they're gettin' turned loose right now.'

Bill slipped from his horse and adjusted his cinch. 'We'll just drop down into the Hole and scout it out on the off chance that they're hidin' there and missed the signal.'

They plowed their way into an area of ancient volcanic eruptions, now eroded into a hodgepodge of deep gully washes and waste land coulees, strewn with piles of loose rock slabs in disordered and irregular arrangement. And everywhere was brush. Sharp-hooked cat's-claw, wispy chaparral bushes, and thorny mesquite tore at their boot-tops and clothing. Cactus lay bunched over the ground like shocks of grain in a heavy field, and bearded spines dug into the horses' forelegs and ankle joints.

As they picked their way, the screech of a bullet ripped through the brush directly in front of them. Simultaneously came the soft pouf! from the explosion of a gun fired in the distance.

'Wasn't far wrong in our first guess,' grinned Bill.

'Git under cover! Git under cover!' yelled Matt, flinging himself to the ground behind a large rock. 'That bullet cut off a twig not more'n a foot from yo'r head!'

Bill pulled his Winchester from its scabbard. 'Come on!' he shouted, plunging through the brush. 'We cain't never catch a cow thief hidin' behind a rock!'

Before they had covered more than a quarter of a mile, they ran onto Sancho and the little bunch of cattle, huddled close together.

'They're around here somewhere,' said Bill. 'Them cattle ain't been turned loose more'n ten minutes.'

'There they go!' interrupted Matt, pointing to a low hogback leading out from the river on the south side.

There was a small man, leaning low over his saddle-horn, riding a snuff-colored brown horse at full speed a half mile away.

'It's Harte all right,' Bill said as he spurred ahead. 'I know that hoss. I saw 'im in his *remuda* last spring. He's what the Mexicans call a *grullo,* and he's the best-lookin' pony that I ever laid eyes on.'

'We ort to be in shootin' distance as soon's we top the divide,' said Matt.

They were now crossing the river and Matt's voice was drowned out by the splashing water.

'Be careful,' Bill warned as their horses struggled up the steep bank. 'We might ride into a ambush. I don't know yet how-come Harte to run away so suddenly, unless he's got a card up his sleeve.'

They climbed to higher ground, and Bill turned and looked over the country they had just left. A mile back of them, he saw a group of twenty men riding into the Devil's Hole.

'That's why he run,' Bill said, pointing to the horsemen. 'He seen them and he thought it was a posse after his scalp.'

'If it is a posse of them farmers,' replied Matt, 'I bet they've got blood in their eye. I'd run too if I thought that crowd was comin' at me.'

'Come on,' Bill said. 'It'd be kind of comfortin' to have them with us, but we ain't got time to wait. The man we're after will be gone long before them fellers git here.'

When they reached the crest of the hill, they could make out a thin queue of dust following in the wake of a man and horse swinging along at half speed, a mile away.

'Don't look very encouragin' now,' Bill remarked. 'He's on a good hoss that's been restin' all day and he's ridin' light as a feather. Our ponies've been under saddle since midnight and are leg-weary — but anyhow — we'll give 'im a run for his money'; and he broke into a swift gallop.

But now, good fortune seemed to be with the inspectors. They were cutting across the ruts of a worn trail, and sighted a man driving four head of loose saddle horses along.

'How-dee-doo!' shouted Bill. 'This is luck. We'll git some rested hossflesh if we have to hogtie a waddie to do it.'

Bill ordered Matt to halt the horses which were trotting along ahead of their driver, and he dashed up to the man.

'We want a couple of fresh hosses, pardner,' Bill said hurriedly to a short-legged, round-faced fat man, and the two eyed each other.

He closed one eye and glanced wisely at Bill with a side twist of his head. 'Yeah?' he grunted. 'They's lots of fellers in yo'r same fix. My advice to you is to go somewhere they've got hosses for sale and buy some.'

'Listen, pardner!' interrupted Bill. 'We're chasin' a cow thief. Our ponies is give out. We want some fresh ones. Savvy? We're brand inspectors. Them hosses is branded Rocking Chair. Yo'r boss is a member of the brand association.'

'Well, why'n the hell didn't you say so?' the Rocking Chair cowboy spat out. 'Now, if I figgered on makin' a long journey, why, I'd pick either that long-legged sorrel, or that blaze-faced black——'

'I'll take the sorrel,' interrupted Bill, flinging his loop around the sorrel horse's head, while Matt roped the black.

'Take our ponies to the ranch with you,' Bill ordered. He tightened his cinch. 'We'll be there some time durin' the night. If we don't catch this feller before dark, the jig's up.'

The *grullo* horse and its rider had now passed from sight over a low ridge. By the time Bill and Matt regained sight of him, he was traveling along at a slow gait and was little further ahead than he was at the time they stopped to change horses.

'He's givin' his pony a chance to blow. He'll need it too when we git lined out. We're goin' to make Mister Harte look like he's standin' still.'

Before they had covered another mile, Bill decided that his enthusiasm had been misplaced. They hit a swinging run at half speed, but the *grullo* horse stayed an even distance ahead and kept just out of gunshot range.

For the remainder of the evening the race carried on until the fresh horses weakened from the burning contest. But not so with the *grullo*. He swept along at the same steady gait, and appeared to Bill to be as fresh as when the chase started.

At sundown, the two inspectors pulled their winded horses to a stop. Three quarters of a mile ahead, they saw the *grullo* mounting one of the hogbacks jutting out from Brady Mountain. Within a few minutes he disappeared from sight among a fringe of live oak brush and the gathering dusk.

'What a horse! What a horse!' Bill sighed with a tremor of emotion in his voice. 'Wouldn't I like to own 'im, though! If I did, a thousand dollars wouldn't touch 'im,' he finished.

Bill patted his exhausted horse on the neck while he loosened his cinch. 'You've done well, ol' boy,' he said. 'But we've got to own that we've been overmatched. We'll have to call it a day.'

Bill swung into his saddle and led off on a straight line for the Rocking Chair headquarters. As they rode along, he voiced more of his thoughts.

'It won't do no good for us to follow Harte to his ranch and arrest 'im for stealin' Sancho and them other cattle. Neither one of us could go into court and swear for certain he was with the cattle. The Baxter boy says he cain't identify any of the men neither. The sheriff and prosecutin' attorney has both told me that identity must be definite and certain, or some such high-flutin' words, before we can expect a conviction in court.'

'Maybe we could find the cook and the other feller who was with Harte,' suggested Matt.

"Twouldn't do no good neither,' replied Bill. 'We never saw them around the cattle. Harte is the only one we had a chance at, and we lost him.'

Bill shifted wearily in his saddle as they came to the Rocking Chair ranch at midnight.

'We've had a pretty long stretch to lose out in the end, Mattie,' he said. 'But don't be discouraged. We'll git another chance at Harte. He'll be back through here with a herd next spring, and he cain't help but steal cattle. We'll just spread our loops and have 'em ready to drag 'im in when he sidesteps and gits a cow that ain't his'n.'

CHAPTER TWELVE
'PREPARE FOR A LAWSUIT, MACK'

THE group of horsemen riding down into the Devil's Hole were indeed a posse of farmers, organized to recover their stolen cattle. They stumbled upon the little bunch of tired animals and started them home, and after a consultation they decided to leave Sancho in this strange land and rid themselves of him forever.

Thus a concerted effort among them succeeded in cutting Sancho out. He was too tired and leg-weary to resist with speed, but instead he employed his cunning. When the farmers abandoned him and returned to their own cattle, he remained discreetly behind. But just the same, when they arrived home, late at night, he lay down among his mates of the farm.

The cattle Bill Sanders cut from the trail herds and turned loose upon the open range caused the Red Bank neighborhood to be overstocked, and serious inroads were made upon the supply of grass. When frost came and stopped the growth of range feed, Sancho again felt the pangs of hunger. Perhaps he remembered some very delicious feed of a farm in the days gone by. Coincidentally, came the memory of painful experiences as an aftermath of invading a farm. Therefore he held shyly aloof from the temptation for some time.

After watching the domestic cattle enjoy their food, Sancho's hunger took control of will-power and he fell before the tempting fragrance of cured feed in the stalk fields and stack lots. When he tried to follow other cattle into the fields and the farmers denied him admission, he simply circled around and broke through the fence at a convenient and safe place.

His fence-breaking depredations brought down upon his head the hostility of all farmers, and they and their dogs gave him much annoyance, but in time he learned to take care of himself.

He found that farmers usually traveled on foot, and it was easy to keep away from the sticks and rocks they hurled. When they were mounted, their slow horses could be easily outrun in the brush and over rough ground. The dogs were not lost so easily, but he learned that they too were far from the dangerous animals they seemed to be. No matter how vicious and daring when backed up by the presence of their masters, they lost much of their courage when alone. By leading them away from the men, a quick whirl and a thrust with his one horn would send them scampering back to cover. Thus he became notorious as a fence-breaking outlaw, and he was dogged and chased from every farm in the community.

When the wrath of the farmers and their dogs made things too hot for him, Sancho would retreat to the freedom of the open range, where he learned to supplement the dry grass with the evergreen mistletoe which grew in clusters from tree limbs. He learned to rear up and stick his long neck high into the foliage, which brought much of this food within reach.

Upon a crisp day in January, he located a large cluster. It hung from a limb above the fork of a leaning tree. It was unapproachable from one side, and a narrow backbone of hard ground between two gully washes made approach difficult from the other. Sancho mounted the narrow strip of ground and walked to the tree. He reared up and licked out his tongue for a bite of food. The ground caved from under his foot and he came down, with his neck lodged in the tree fork. His feet were resting upon solid ground now, but his head was held so high that it was impossible for him to dislodge it.

He pulled and bucked his hardest, but he only fastened himself tighter. The fire of battle flashed from his eyes, and he bellowed with rage, but no human being chanced by to give him help.

For five days Sancho stood locked in his painful position. His struggles at last became weak twistings of hips and back. His flashing eyes grew dim in luster and receded deeply into their sockets. His hide drew tight around shrinking flanks, and a slimy ooze dripped from mouth and nostrils. Low moans of pain were the only sounds that came from his swelling throat.

Upon the fifth day a dim apparition floated into his line of blurred vision. This thing seemed to be surrounded by a mist of colors, and as Sancho blinked watery eyes, a woman in a bright red coat and a blue sunbonnet stood looking upon him with horror.

She ran hurriedly away, and within a few minutes two forms appeared. The other was a man with an axe who swung a few well-directed blows, and one side of the tree fork toppled to the ground. When the severed half fell away, Sancho lifted his head slowly and painfully from the stock. Chunks of decomposed hide and flesh peeled from his neck and clung to the tree bark.

The dazed steer now glared at his liberators with dull eyes. The woman stepped forward and started to pat his head. Sancho imagined another enemy stood before him and he lunged fiercely toward her. The stiffened muscles and joints of his body refused to obey his crazed brain and the thrust of his horn went amiss, but the weight of his body knocked his intended victim to the ground. Bellowing with rage, he staggered around and tried to lower his head and drive his one horn into the still body.

The man recovered from his shock, and struck Sancho a hard blow upon the head with the axe butt. An overwhelming darkness folded around him and he pitched head-first to the ground.

His knotted legs twisted under and the point of his nose half-buried itself in a gathering of dry silt in the ravine bottom.

When a doctor was called to treat the injured woman, the news spread over the sparsely settled countryside. Before the physician emerged from the tent which housed the patient, a crowd had gathered.

Many of them went to the scene and found the emaciated steer resting sullenly upon his haunches. At their approach, he struggled to his feet and reeled out of sight into the brush. To those living in the community, he was a familiar figure. To others he was known by reputation, and a former employee of the Tree Top entertained the crowd by reciting his life history.

When the Old Hoss heard of the affair, he went at once to make amends. The injured woman, he learned, was the wife of one Marcus Hulen, a civil engineer with headquarters in Chicago. They were camped in a surveying party running out the line of a proposed railroad. When he inquired for Hulen, he learned that the couple had departed for Chicago. The Old Hoss was greatly worried, and he made the fatal blunder of expressing himself in a letter to Hulen, in which he acknowledged all blame and laid it to negligence of himself and his men for permitting such a dangerous animal to roam at large among a community of people.

Hulen was well posted in the rule of law governing liability for personal injury. Therefore, when he learned that the steer was owned by the reputed wealthy cattleman, he could visualize a handsome monetary return for damages, and he laid his plans accordingly.

The Old Hoss never heard from Hulen directly. He received a letter from a firm of Chicago lawyers demanding an immediate payment of twenty-five thousand dollars, with a threat of filing suit for a larger amount. Then he went to consult a local attorney, who advised him to settle the case out of court.

The Old Hoss arose from his chair and nervously paced the floor. 'It's robbery, just plain robbery, and I won't pay them a damned cent. I'd have spent twenty-five thousand dollars with a good grace if it had taken that much to put that woman back in good health; but this is robbery.'

He paused in his harangue and looked inquiringly at the silent lawyer. Receiving no reply, he resumed: 'I don't know much law — never paid much attention to such things. I always paid what I owed and let the other go. They'll have to sue me here at home, won't they? My friends will never stand for me to be robbed in such a fashion.'

The lawyer leaned back in his chair and smiled indulgently at his troubled client. He tapped the open palm of his hand with the blade of a letter-opener.

'Perhaps so and perhaps not,' he said. 'There might be some law on jurisdiction that you've never heard about. This case is not likely to come up for trial here among your friends. There is a recently enacted federal statute that permits a resident of one state to sue a resident of another, in the nearest federal court of jurisdiction. It is my opinion that they will avail themselves of this privilege.'

'We'll give 'em a run for their money in any court in the land,' the Old Hoss snapped, with his short mustache rising to a bristle. 'I've never let a gang of robbers bamboozle me into anything yet, and I don't intend to start now. I'll fight this case to a finish if it takes every cow that wears the Tree Top brand to do it. You had just as well prepare yourself for a lawsuit, Mack.'

CHAPTER THIRTEEN

THE HOLIDAY PICNIC

S ANCHO fought a desperate and uphill battle for life. His body throbbed with dull aches from his horns to the tip of his tail. The pain of stiffened neck joints varied with the weather, and he often chose to go hungry rather than undergo the torture of raising and lowering his head to graze. He browsed moodily over stale and trampled grass stubs along the watercourse rather than tax his sore muscles by walking back for fresher grazing.

His daring spirit lapsed into a timid fear, and he no longer braved the wrath of farmers and their dogs. The most courage he could muster was to stand shyly at a safe distance and beg with those dim and wistful eyes, and the only reward he received for his begging was cruel abuse when he ventured too close. Not one of the farmers took pity and threw a single bunch of hay or a stalk of feed toward him. On the contrary, the dogs appeared to sense his weakened condition, and made their attacks with more viciousness than they would have dared in times past.

With everything against him, Sancho retreated into the solitude of brush which was the only place of safety he knew. He found for his hideout a heavy grove of pecan trees lining the north side of Red Bank Creek. In despondency he saw the break of winter and the forerunners of spring as early buds started to swell in February.

His retreat was only a short distance from the Red Bank community schoolhouse where it nestled in its setting of oak trees upon a low bench, jutting out from a chain of hills flanking the creek valley. Since its organization, the school had never permitted the twenty-second of February to pass without paying tribute to the Father of His Country. When weather permitted, the celebration took the form of an outdoor picnic.

The school was composed of only one slender young lady as instructor, and a student body of just seventeen awkward and shy boys and girls of varying ages, but the spirit of patriotism burned earnestly in their hearts. Therefore, the teacher assembled her array of juvenile protégés with bulging lunch baskets upon the memorable day and led them forth to celebrate the occasion.

The gay crowd arrived at the chosen spot for the picnic, which, unfortunately, was situated in a grove of large pecan trees upon the north side of the Red Bank. A place to spread the tablecloths was cleared of entangling brush and sticks. The lunch baskets were then placed ready for unpacking.

Had a dietitian glimpsed the contents of those baskets, she would likely have been horrified, but a hungry person would have returned a fervent thanks for the food blessing. There were pans of downy biscuits, still fresh and warm with oven heat; links of richly seasoned sausages and slabs of cured ham; hunks of tender roast beef, bowls of salad, and ricks and piles of fried chicken; baked potato yams; and an assortment of pies and pans of layer cake, dripping with their rich filling.

While the table was being spread, a pair of red-rimmed eyes watched with hate and increasing anger through a screen of heavy brush, and a low bellow went unnoticed by the jubilant group.

The boys had set the flagpole. The halyard was threaded into a leather loop at the top and two sturdy boys stood ready to hoist away on signal. The teacher had grouped the assemblage around her, and she stood facing the flag with a book of patriotic essays in her hand, ready to pay fitting tribute to the emblem.

A gust of wind caught the sagging flag and whipped it around broadside to the pair of watching eyes. The broad red stripes melted into a solid field of taunting color to the blurred vision. With all his pent-up rage surging forth, Sancho lowered his head and charged into the group.

The startled children broke and fled before his bellowing charge. The teacher flung the younger ones into convenient trees, and she too clambered to an undignified position astride a limb, barely ahead of Sancho's horn.

After his intended victims escaped, Sancho went for the red stripes of the flag where it hung breast-high. When nothing remained but the broken staff and tatters of colored cloth, he turned toward the luncheon spread. While he pawed across the table and hooked the lunch baskets one way and another, he was suddenly interrupted.

At the thuds of a running horse's feet and the crack of breaking brush behind him, he swung around, and what he saw turned him away in full flight. A horse had broken into the clearing. Upon its back rode Bill Sanders. He was loosening the coils of his rope as he came.

When the season for trail herds was over, Bill returned to the ranch to spend the winter. He knew that no cattle would be moving before the middle of March, but nevertheless, a full month earlier found him preparing to leave for his post of duty. Bill had been hearing rumors from the direction of Coleman Town. A stray wisp of gossip informed him that the teacher in the Red Bank school had resigned and that a niece of 'Doc' Lowe's from Fort Worth had been appointed to fill the vacancy.

And back to Coleman Town went Bill. A few guarded inquiries verified the rumor, and he rode out to the Red Bank the day of the picnic to see for himself.

'Sancho, you old trouble-makin' reprobate,' he swore as his horse came alongside — and for the first time, Bill struck Sancho by slashing his back with a doubled rope. 'You've got ever'body down on you in the country,' Bill continued, 'and now you keep on with devilment until you strain my own patience to the breakin' point.'

Bill again snapped the end of his rope along the steer's side with such force that it raised small bunches of hair, and he saw Sancho's back and hips twist in pain.

'Ain't we got trouble enough without you stirrin' up more all time?' he asked. 'Some of these days, you're goin' to meet up with a match that you cain't git out of. If you don't behave, you're goin' to git a Winchester ball planted right square between them big eyes of yo'rn, and then all we'll have to remember you by will be yo'r hide stretched over a fence.'

With another healthy cut at the awkwardly galloping steer, Bill rode back to appraise the amount of damage. Some of the most venturesome boys were emerging from their places of retreat. The teacher still clung to her place on the tree, her little feet furiously kicking the air as she squirmed in a frantic effort to disengage one side of her skirt from a snag above her head, and at the same time stretch the dress to cover her legs. At Bill's approach, she flung herself from the perch, and her fall was accompanied by the sound of ripping cloth. She regained her feet and her clothing settled into place, but there was a rent halfway up her skirt and a strip of pink gingham trailed upon the ground.

When she turned her face toward him, a flutter arose in Bill's breast. Brown hair tumbled in confusion over the side of her head. A crushed sunbonnet dangled unevenly from the ends of its strings knotted around her neck. Her blouse rose and fell spasmodically with deep breathing and she trembled from emotion and exertion. Her eyes flashed in a mixture of dismay and anger.

Yes, there was no mistake. It was the same girl. Bill could remember the time he had seen those eyes flash before, but he was glad that her anger was directed toward poor old Sancho instead of himself.

'Looks sort of like you've been treed,' Bill said with a broad grin, dismounting in front of her.

She looked at the bright threads of cloth hanging to the knotty snag above. She surveyed the torn dress and a crimson flooded her face. She raised her head toward Bill and their eyes met and held steady. They stood thus for an instant, and then the tension broke and they both laughed.

'I — I — don't know how to thank you,' she said. 'You happened along at a fortunate time. My name is Virginia Lowe'; and she extended her hand.

Bill felt a little disappointment in the greeting. He wanted her to recognize him. Could it be that she didn't? Then he suddenly hoped it to be so. He could start all over again. Still, she would have to know some time. He might just as well get it over with now.

'Not a-tall. Not a-tall,' he managed to stammer from his mixed thoughts. 'You don't owe me no thanks. My name's Sanders — we've met before.'

A shadow passed over Virginia's face and a frown lingered on her brow. Then her face brightened.

'Oh — oh. Are you? Are you? I remember now!' she hurried to say.

'That's Bill Sanders,' piped the shrill voice of ten-year-old Lonnie Mason. 'I've seen 'im lots of times. My pap says he's the best cowhand and brand inspector in the whole state of Texas, and he ain't afraid of hell fire neither.'

The youthful enthusiast stopped suddenly with a brand of guilt upon his face. The reproof he had learned to expect from his impulsive outbreak into swear words was not forthcoming — but an uneasy conscience was already at work.

'I — I ain't talkin' that way myself, Miss Virginia — I'm jus' tellin' what Pap said.'

During the outburst of his young admirer, Bill had a feeling that the conversation was getting too personal. An ocean of humility was sweeping upon him. Now that he had found the very time and opportunity he had been looking forward to, he could not face the music and was ready to run. He lifted the bridle reins over his horse's head, and grasped the short mane in front of the animal's withers.

'I guess I'd better be goin' now,' he said.

He laid his right hand upon the saddle horn and placed his left foot in the stirrup.

'I'm glad there wasn't nobody hurt. You won't be bothered any more. When I git through that steer will be so far away it'll take 'im a week to git back——'

'Mr. Sanders,' interrupted Virginia, stepping nearer, 'won't you stay and have lunch with us — that is, if that beast hasn't destroyed it all? It wouldn't be treating us right to run off and leave us now.'

Bill looked around helplessly at the group of silent children and their expectant faces. 'Yes'm,' he said, returning his attention to Virginia. 'I'd like mighty well to have dinner with you all, but' — he hesitated — 'it's been a long time since I et with women folks — I've been sort of used to scrappin' for what I git to eat in a cow camp.'

'If that's all that is bothering you,' laughed the girl, 'it's settled right now. We'll dispense with every formality.'

Bill found a comfortable seat by the side of Virginia. He never overburdened her with conversation, but he did manage to declare that he was eating the best meal and having the best time of his life. But soon he was again perturbed over one of Sancho's acts.

A five-year-old child who enjoyed the distinction of being the baby and favorite of the crowd came to her teacher in deep sobs. In her hands she carried a battered cake pan. In the pan were the remains of a layer cake, now mashed into a dirty paste with the imprint of Sancho's hoof in the center. Again Bill saw the flash of fire come into Virginia's eyes while she comforted the weeping child.

'I hate to think of brutality,' she murmured, 'but that animal should be killed.'

'Yes'm,' Bill admitted grudgingly. 'Yes'm, I guess you're right. Here of late he's got to be a right bothersome sort of a steer — but — but somehow, I kind of feel sorry for 'im. You see when he was a little calf I——'

As Bill leaned against the bole of a tree and told the story of Sancho's life, all his diffidence and former shyness departed. Words came easily, and he no longer felt the strain of embarrassment. He watched his listener, and noted with satisfaction that a changed expression was creeping upon her face. He warmed to his subject at finding such a desirable person to share a common view with him. When he finished, the girl's eyes were soft with moisture and she avoided his gaze.

'Poor thing,' she almost whispered in a voice that trilled with emotion. 'I never thought that so much pathos could be connected with an animal's life. I think it is good and noble for you to keep faith in him. Now, I'd hate to see a single hair harmed on his body. I hope you take good care of him the rest of his life.'

'I aim to,' said Bill warmly. 'I'm glad you feel the way I do. I don't know anybody else that does — since all the trouble he's got into.'

While he was talking, Bill had been tossing his pearl-handled pocket knife from one hand to the other. Now he laid it upon his doubled leg to roll a cigarette. A twist of his knee sent it sliding to the ground, and the girl watched it disappear in a carpet of dry leaves and grass.

Before Bill realized it, the sun was dropping behind the tall trees, reminding him that it was time for the picnic crowd to be going home.

'It certainly has been a pleasure to meet you again,' Virginia said as Bill prepared to leave. 'We are having a little gathering at my schoolhouse next Saturday night, and everybody concerned would be glad to have you there.'

'Yes'm,' Bill replied with his broad grin. 'I've always been sort of woman-shy, but now I feel as if I know you. I'll be at yo'r schoolhouse next Saturday night, or bust a hobble. In the meantime, don't you forget' — he reddened suddenly at the thought of his intended next words — 'about pore old Sancho.' He stepped into the stirrup, swung into his saddle, and rode away.

Virginia stood watching until he and his horse faded from sight behind a screen of brush. She knelt and delved among the leaves. She picked up a small pearl-handled knife, turned it over slowly, slipped it into her purse, and snapped the lock.

CHAPTER FOURTEEN
FREDDIE WILLIAMS
APPEARS

After his new start with Virginia, Bill did not waste any time by letting their friendship lag. The thoughts that had been lurking in the back of his mind for so long were now unfolding into reality. The Washington's Birthday picnic was not the last visit he made to the Red Bank schoolhouse. He fulfilled his promise to attend the party, and many times after that he found excuses for being in that vicinity, and he timed himself to arrive at or near the dismissal hour and walk with Virginia to the farmhouse where she boarded. On other occasions he would lead another horse and take her for long rides over the cattle range.

Thus, upon a day a month after their meeting, Bill led an extra saddle horse toward the schoolhouse. A deep frown creased his forehead under his hat brim and his jaws were set in determination. He twisted nervously from one side of his saddle to the other and his voice intoned certain words as if he were reading them from a book.

'Virginia,' he would mumble. 'I have a very serious matter to talk to you about. I realize that you might think it strange coming from me, but for a long time I have had this feeling, but I ain't got — ah, shucks!' he would say, and then start all over again.

When he arrived, his determination was melting away and he compromised with himself by putting off the main purpose of his visit until later. As twilight drew on they rode along through the creeping shadows, and Bill lapsed into a deep silence as he tried to assemble the words of his intended speech. Again he decided to procrastinate until they reached Virginia's home, where he would have the inspiration from the moonlight.

When they arrived, Bill helped her from the horse and he held tightly to her arms at the elbows. He stood peering intently into her upturned eyes and saw the moon reflect a faint surprise in their blue depths.

'I've got somethin' to say — and I don't know where to start in at,' he said hoarsely, which was not at all like what he had planned to say.

Virginia drew away and took a step backward. She turned her head aside and her face was hidden from Bill's view. After waiting an eternity for her to speak, Bill marshaled all his shrinking courage for one desperate try. He stepped impulsively ahead and recovered his hold upon her arms and drew her to him. She pulled one hand free and held it up before him in a staying gesture.

'Please — please,' she begged and her eyes repeated the spoken entreaty when they looked once more into his own.

On the instant Bill felt the ground crumbling under his feet and he knew he had dropped his chance.

'I'm sorry,' he said gruffly, trying to cover his wild desire to curse his awkwardness and ill luck. 'I've been on the wrong side of the fence all the time and didn't know it. I haven't got any right to think you'd feel the same way I do. We ain't the same kind of people and I ain't fit to walk in the dirt while you ride along — but I hope you'll overlook me aimin' my shot at the stars.'

Virginia stepped to Bill's side and put her hand upon his arm. She looked into his face and he saw a teardrop hovering upon her lower lashes.

'She feels sorry for me,' Bill thought; then she spoke in a clear voice that carried a tinge of rebuke.

'Please don't say those things — they hurt. It's not that way. I just didn't expect — I must have time to think.'

'Then there's not some feller back where you come from?' Bill asked anxiously.

Virginia slid her fingers down his arm until they closed upon his broad hand. She lifted it and held it gently in both her own.

'No,' she said in soft but positive tones. 'There is no one anywhere.'

She gave his hand a squeeze and dropped it. She then ran hurriedly through the gate and into the house.

Bill looked down at the hand she had held in blank wonder. How long he stood thus he did not know, but a jerk reminded him that he was holding the reins of two hungry horses in his numb fingers.

He turned slowly and mounted his horse. So entranced he was upon his return trip, the time and distance never came within his thoughts.

The days that followed were the happiest of Bill's entire life. Before he knew it March had run into April, and he sensed more from intuition and habit than from thought that things were beginning to happen. The coming events to which he had always looked forward with zealous anticipation held little interest for him now. The most of his thoughts ran back to a slender girl who presided over a small classroom in a little white schoolhouse, sitting upon a low bench of ground in the Red Bank valley.

All conversation in saloons and upon street corners was being directed toward range affairs, while booted men with jingling spurs upon their heels hustled around in preparation for the coming work. Bill heard this conversation as from a distance, but took little part in it. He knew that cattle were breaking out from winter seclusion and that saddle horses were being massed together for the general spring round-up. He realized in a subconscious way that far to the south, in the early grass country of the Gulf Coast and Rio Grande, great herds of long-horned steers destined to pass his brand inspection were already on the trail and moving toward him on their long drive to the northern markets.

With the knowledge that only a few precious days remained before work would claim all his time, he felt a dislike at being deprived of these few days when a process-server handed him a subpoena which commanded his presence as a witness in Fort Worth, where opposing forces were already gathering for a desperate court battle.

But before the time came for him to leave for court a far worse situation presented itself. A stylishly dressed young man, whom Virginia introduced to every one as Freddie Williams and a life-long friend, had appeared upon the scene. Then the ugly head of doubt and uncertainty rose above its coils and struck hard at Bill's happiness.

When the Old Hoss appeared in Federal Court to answer the damage action brought by Hulen, both he and his caravan of picturesque witnesses added interest to the already noted case. The Fort Worth papers gave it much publicity and ran exaggerated feature stories of Sancho. Down in the Coleman country where the convalescing steer hid in the brush, he developed into a good source of revenue for the local photographer. When the trial was over, the Old Hoss returned and gave voice to his disgust at the notoriety.

'Get that steer back to the ranch and out of my sight forever, if you have to cut him into pieces and take one piece at a time,' he ordered Bill Sanders in strong language. 'If we don't get rid of him this spring somehow, I'll fire every man on the ranch and start all over again. I'm sick of all this monkey business.'

Thus, once more Sancho found mounted men upon his trail, when Bill Sanders and Matt Cook routed him from his haunts on the Red Bank.

Sancho bore slight resemblance to the staggering, fighting animal that had broken up the picnic. He was already feeling the effects of early grass, and snorted his contempt of mankind by clattering away through the brush. But he overestimated his own prowess and underestimated the determination of his trailers. The two cowboys rode hard after him, and before sunset on the fifth day of April he plunged across the Colorado into his native range, where he became lost among the thousands of other Tree Top cattle.

Bud West sat with the back of his chair propped against the wall in the large dining-room at the Tree Top ranch. An oil lamp hanging in a bracket above his head cast dim rays over the shadowy room. Spread across his lap was the latest issue of the *Democrat,* Coleman Town's four-page weekly paper, where the editor had sacrificed much boiler-plate advertising to make space for a detailed report of Sancho and his escapades. Dave Houston, Bob Long, and three other men sat at a table, absorbed in the ranch pastime of poker-playing. In the kitchen, Nig hummed a wailing chant to the clatter of supper dishes.

'That beats the deuce both ways from the jack,' exclaimed Bud, as he folded up the paper and laid it carefully upon the floor. 'After all them shenanigans and goin' ons, we're all right back where we started from. Sancho's back on the range. The Old Hoss'll soon be here. That court found that Hulen's wife has still got her good health and wa'n't hurt none by Sancho, and Banjy still prods us fellers out of bed before daylight.'

'Who win'd that dar co'te case, mistah Bud?' asked Nig from the kitchen doorway, with a dishcloth flung over his shoulder.

'We win,' replied Bud. He threw back his head and hooked a thumb in the armhole of his vest. 'This here paper tells all about it. Jus' listen to what it says about the Old Hoss. It says:

'"Mr. Denman completely captivated the jury by his openly frank manner and direct honesty. His convincing sincerity truly pictured his noble character." If the rest of you simple-minded cow hands cain't handle them four-bit, jaw-breakin' words, they mean that the Old Hoss is a A number one guy that plays his cards straight across the table, and the jury could read his hand. I bet the ol' boy steps high wide and handsome when he reads all that good news about hisself. While he's feelin' like a playful colt, he's liable to give us a raise in wages.'

'Give us a raise! Give us a raise!' scoffed Dave Houston. 'He's most apt to give you a raise from behind with the toe of his boot. It ain't goin' to be healthy for any cowhand that makes him think about that steer.'

'Is he out for cowhands' scalps?' asked Bob Long, shoving a stack of chips into the pot and raising an inquiring eyebrow at the player on his left.

'Worse'n that,' explained Dave, throwing his hand into the discard. 'I heard 'im explode in town the other day, and I don't think scalps'll satisfy 'im any more. He wants the whole hide now.'

'Shore, shore,' agreed Bud. 'He's got his skinnin' knife sharpened for one feller in this outfit, but it ain't me. If a certain waddie that ain't so very far away at this minute had been as attentive to ol' Sancho as he was to the long-whiskered farmer's gal down on the river, Sancho'd never have got into all this mess.'

'Hold on, there. Hold on, there, mister big mouth. You're liable to overjump,' warned Dave with flushed cheeks. 'You'll leave my personal affairs out of this if you know what's healthy for you.'

'What does Bill Sanders have to say about Sancho and the court trial?' asked Bob Long.

'Bill's sort of like the little boy that the calf run over,' responded Dave Houston, with a glare at Bud West. 'He ain't got nothin' to say. He's got troubles of his own. He took out a hand with the little schoolmarm down on the Red Bank. For awhile the cards fell his way, but they say around Coleman Town that another feller's horned in at the table and slipped in a cold deck on Bill.'

Bud West slid his chair over and took a position facing Dave. He placed his elbows upon the table and cupped his chin in his hands. A fleeting smile played around the corners of Dave's mouth, pleased at Bud's apparent agitation, and he continued with his narrative.

'This here feller that broke into Bill's game is a dude. He hit town about a month ago and got a job in the bank. He's got wavy hair, parts it in the middle, and goes dressed up like a hoss on parade. He's keepin' the road hot between Coleman Town and the Red Bank schoolhouse. They say that he's got the bulge in the race and he's just about got Bill pushed onto the turf. I guess that's about right, too. Bill ain't got no chance agin a slick-haired banker.'

'And that's about enough out of you,' snarled Bud. 'You cain't stand any gaff when it's comin' at you, but you're handy when it comes to dealin' off the bottom of the deck about other fellers — especially when they ain't here to take their part.'

'That don't count,' retorted Dave. 'I ain't sayin' nothin' derogatory — as I heard one of them lawyers say over at Fort Worth. Besides, if you don't like it — you know what you can do.'

'I don't like it!' shouted Bud. 'And one more bark out of you about Bill Sanders you'll find me straddle of yo'r neck——'

'Git straddle of my neck!' roared Dave. 'If you do there won't nobody have to tell you to git off.'

Bob Long arose and swept the deck of cards together and placed them in their box.

'You ducks make me sick,' he said. 'Come on and sleep it off.'

CHAPTER FIFTEEN

A LITTLE JOB FOR THE DEPUTY SHERIFF

ACK in Coleman Town, the spring drive was passing and Bill's work was pushing him like a slave from early dawn until late at night. He realized that Fred Williams, the bank clerk, was drinking too much and running with the wrong crowd for a man of his station. Virginia did not seem to be acquainted with the other side of his character. Bill tried to bury himself in work and let things go, but Virginia remained uppermost in his thoughts in spite of his dogged resolution to stay away from the Red Bank schoolhouse.

It was late one night in April when Bill stopped in town on his way to camp, tied his horse in front of the Exchange Saloon, and to his surprise saw Virginia coming down the board sidewalk toward him.

'I've been waiting for you, and I'm so glad to see you,' she said in tones that set Bill's heart to pounding. 'I want you to do something for me.'

'I'll do anything — for you,' he stammered.

'Mr. Williams,' Virginia hurried to say, 'is in that horrible place over the Silver Dollar Saloon. Please get him out of there.'

As Bill's mouth opened in amazement the girl hurried on, 'You said you'd do anything.'

THE TRAIL BOSS

'Y-e-s-m,' he mumbled, 'but you've cut out a sort of a funny job. Williams is a man of his own, and I figure he can come and go as he pleases. In this country, we don't ever bother nobody till he bothers somebody else.'

'But you don't understand,' she begged. 'Freddie is not himself. He isn't responsible.'

'I cain't help that,' Bill objected stubbornly. 'I ain't in the habit of hornin' into other feller's affairs. Besides, them friends of his'n are set in their ways, and they might object to me comin' in there to drag a customer out of the place.'

'Oh,' she said hotly. 'So your quick promise meant nothing.'

She turned away, but not before Bill caught the glisten of a tear on her cheek.

'Wait!' he commanded. 'If you want that feller, I'll go in there and bring 'im out if I have to wreck the house to do it. Where do you want 'im brought to?'

Virginia raised her head and smiled gratitude through shining eyes. She clasped Bill's hand between both of her own.

The hand and fingers that were so deft and precise at twirling ropes and wreathing cinch straps felt large and clumsy and awkwardly out of place now. Bill pulled his hand from her grasp and walked away. With the pressure of her fingers still warm upon his own, he mounted the rickety stairs leading to the place above the Silver Dollar Saloon.

Bill opened the door upon a medium-sized room. The interior reeked with the stench of liquor and stale tobacco. Thick layers of smoke floated in the heavy atmosphere like streaks of moss in stagnant water. A lamp hung from a gaudy chandelier and cast ringed shadows over a gambling table.

In the dealer's chair was a heavy-jowled man in loud dress. A green eyeshade rested low upon his forehead, hiding the upper part of his face. In front of him were ricks of poker chips and stacks of silver dollars. Weighted down by one stack of coin was a flat slip of paper. The upper side bore the printed head of BANK

DRAFT. In the lower right-hand corner which edged from under the weights, Bill could see the scrawled signature 'F. W. Williams.'

Upon the dealer's right sat a half-breed, showing strong negroid characteristics. An old scar beginning at the base of his jaw curved upward like an inverted half circle and buried itself amid a heavy mustache under his right nostril. Beady black eyes scowled down a flat nose which overhung a pair of beefy lips. Bill knew the man around Coleman Town as official bouncer of the gambling place, and he was commonly called 'the Indian.'

Upon the dealer's left sat a stranger to Bill, dressed like a cowboy. Directly across the table from the dealer slouched Freddie Williams, leaning upon an elbow with a stupid leer on his face. The dealer leaned back in his chair and placed an open hand upon the stack of money.

'What d'ye want here?' he rasped, tilting his head sidewise and exposing a large red nose and a pair of yellow eyes.

'I want this feller,' Bill replied crisply. He grasped Freddie by the shoulder without taking his eyes from the dealer's face. 'And this,' he said shortly, leaning over the table and jerking the bank draft from under the stack of dollars, scattering them upon the floor.

'I don' want to go anywhere,' protested Freddie.

The blood ebbed from the dealer's face, leaving an ashen pallor of rage. 'I know you're some kind of a jack-leg, pistol-totin' deputy sheriff,' he grated, 'but that don't give you license to come in here and rifle my bank roll. Now you hand me back that draft and take yer hands off that man before I knock you down and stomp you through the floor.'

While the dealer talked, Bill's fingers crawled up to the back of Freddie's collar. He now yanked the bank clerk from his chair and turned toward the head of the stairway, where he found the Indian blocking the way.

'Get aside!' Bill commanded, and the Indian's reply was to strike at Bill's face. Bill ducked the blow, and as he came up he struck out with his free hand, which landed squarely upon the Indian's flat nose. While the Indian staggered, Bill swung Freddie to the landing, and with his foot he gave a strong push which sent him sliding and bumping down the stairs. He now turned to face the Indian, who was coming at him in a weaving crouch, a dirk knife gripped in his right hand.

Bill grasped the chair recently vacated by Freddie and brought it down upon the Indian's head. The legs and rungs cracked like dead tree limbs and the seat was wrenched from the back bows. The Indian's knees buckled under, and his heavy body sagged until it came to an easy rest upon the floor. Bill whirled toward the other two men, and saw the dealer pulling out a drawer from the table, and in the act of lifting a small pistol from it. Bill had no time to reach for his own gun, but with a quick motion he hurled the chair back, striking the dealer full in the face. He keeled backward and lay still. Grasping another chair, Bill turned to the stranger, who sat unmoved.

'How much of this do you want?' Bill asked shortly.

'Not a bit, pardner,' the man replied. 'I just happened along and set in. They was usin' me as a buffer while they robbed the dude.'

'All right,' said Bill, as the Indian stirred. 'Let's git out of here.'

'Nonh,' replied the stranger, indicating a sizable stack of chips in front of him. 'I got a few dollars invested in these and I aim to cash in. I started out here and I aim to finish up here.'

Bill dropped down the stairway and stood surveying the stupefied bank clerk. He leaned over, caught him by the collar, yanked him to his feet, and slapped a little understanding into his blank mind. He then started towing him onto the board walk.

'You gonna put me in jail, sheriff?' mumbled Freddie.

'No,' replied Bill sharply. 'But I — I'd like to——' Seeing the water trough in the center of the street, in an attitude of stiff determination he propelled his charge to it.

But there he stopped. Virginia was walking hurriedly toward them. His hold relaxed a little and he half turned from his undertaking.

'Hull-o, sweet girl,' sang Freddie.

At this, Bill renewed his determination. He tightened his hold upon Freddie's collar with one hand and grasped his belt with the other. He lifted him clear of the ground and doused him under the water — once, twice, three times.

'You'll kill him!' screamed Virginia. 'Don't do that. Don't do that. Pull him out,' she ordered as she ran up and attempted to thrust Bill aside.

'Here he is,' said Bill, as he hauled Freddie from the trough and splashed both himself and Virginia with water. 'He's not pompered as much as he was, but I'll bet he's soberer. What do you want done with 'im?'

Freddie stood a bedraggled, unnoticed witness, while an enraged girl and a disgusted man faced each other. For a short duration neither spoke. Then Virginia found voice.

'I — I — I — I hate you, Bill Sanders!' she almost screamed. She caught Freddie by the arm and started up the street.

Without a word, Bill turned to where his horse was standing. He threw the reins over the animal's neck and stood ready to mount.

'I think I'd better git drunk too,' he rasped, and took his foot from the stirrup.

His eye caught a bright reflection of his deputy sheriff's badge in the moonlight. He reached up and tore it from his vest lapel. He stepped to the well curb and dropped the badge to the bottom.

'That's settled now,' he said vehemently. 'I'm goin' back to the brush and cactus where I know my way around. I got along all right till I tried to go the gaits of town folks and got my feet all tangled up.'

He again gathered up his bridle reins and mounted. Turning his horse toward the Tree Top range, he tried to frame an excuse that would sound plausible to the Old Hoss for his sudden change of mind. He little knew that Buddie West was at that time riding toward him with a message that would relieve him of the embarrassing necessity of making any explanation.

CHAPTER SIXTEEN
LEAD STEER

Back on the Tree Top, spring activities were in full force. Once more Banjy cocked his hat feather at a jaunty angle, fitted the bows of his short legs around the sides of his horse, and swung his outfit onto the range for another round-up. Once more Sancho was caught in the dragnet of riders as they spread out and combed the hills and valleys of the Lower Mustang. Once more the wily steer found himself the match in speed and skill of man and horse.

While the round-up was being thrown together a gushing shower of rain had fallen, leaving a slippery surface upon the hard-packed ground. It was Banjy who started to cut Sancho from the round-up. Sancho bounded out, and then he turned suddenly and started back. Banjy rode squarely in front of him and blocked his path.

Sancho came to a stop, pawed the ground, and tossed his head defiantly. Banjy's cutting-horse was suddenly alert. The tips of his small ears waved forward and came to rest at a steady point. His sharp eyes watched every motion of Sancho's body. The rims of his nostrils fluttered with soft rolls as he drew deep breaths, shifting his feet, thrusting his open mouth forward against Banjy's restraining hand upon the bridle reins — in his eagerness to enter the contest which he sensed to be coming.

When Sancho took the first step, the horse lunged at him fiercely, and they entered into a closely matched race heading at a quarter angle toward the main herd. The horse gained, and the speeding steer gave way before the pressure. Seeing that he was being outrun and forced away from his goal, Sancho whirled squarely to the right.

The soft ground gave way under the weight of his quick turn, and his hind feet slipped from under him. The horse was beyond Banjy's immediate control and was running too fast to stop or turn aside. His front legs tripped over the half-fallen steer's body, and all three rolled into a mass of twisted flesh.

Sancho was the first to untangle himself, and he lunged unsteadily to his feet and limped away. The horse arose slowly and stood trembling while he regarded his fallen rider. Banjy rolled upon his side and pushed himself to a sitting position. Then, using his hands as a prop, he pushed his weight onto one knee, and placing his left foot forward, he arose to his feet. When he took the first step, his right leg crumpled under his weight and he fell sidewise to the ground again.

Blasts of loud profanity ripped the air as the crew of cowboys gathered around their stricken leader and discovered that his right leg was broken between the knee and ankle. Bloodcurdling maledictions were hurled at poor old Sancho. A dozen kinds of torturous deaths were suggested, and as many different executioners volunteered for the job.

'We'd better kill ourselves and be done with it,' mourned Bud West. He dropped to his knees with open knife and ripped out the stitches of Banjy's boot and removed it from his swelling foot. 'When the Old Hoss gits wind of this, he'll make it so hot for us that we'll all wish we was dead.'

Bob Long hurriedly fashioned a lattice of small sticks into a carrier and slipped it under the broken leg. He grasped one end of the sticks and Bud West bent over to catch the other. Dave Houston and another man locked hands under the injured man's back and formed a pack-saddle with their arms.

Bud stood up, fixed Dave Houston with an accusing eye, and continued. 'Now you-all can see what happens when a fancy loop-twister gits moon-eyed over a farmer gal and don't tend to business.'

'What'd'y mean — lookin' at me?' Dave flared, jerking his arm from under Banjy. 'That's the second time you've made a dirty crack about me. I've warned you once, and now I'm goin' to knock them teeth of yorn down yo'r bull neck.' He took a step toward Bud.

'Stop it!' commanded Bob Long springing between them. 'You're just a couple of fools — tryin' to fight with a man on the ground with a broke leg. Grab hold here and help carry Banjy to a shade. One of you jerk that saddle off and make a head-rest. If I had time, I'd lick you both — but that won't be necessary. When the Old Hoss gits through, he'll have all the fight took out of you.'

'All right,' assented Bud West, 'but I'll tell all you bloodthirsty savages that if you do anything to ol' Sancho, Bill Sanders'll break yo'r necks.'

A man was sent for a rig to move Banjy to the comfort of his bed in the cool shadows of the ranch porch. The next day saw the Old Hoss yearning for the resourceful judgment of Bill Sanders. After studying out his problem of a cow outfit without a competent boss, he called Bud West to one side and gave him a few explicit instructions. Bud went to old Meletone and the two of them rounded up the *remuda*. Bud cast his rope upon his toughest circle horse, saddled the animal, and rode away. While Bill Sanders was in the act of tearing the star of deputy sheriff from his vest, Bud was riding into Coleman Town with word for Bill to report at once to the ranch for duty.

Bill Sanders received his orders with the joy that he supposed a man would feel upon being released from bondage. His reaction was too manifest for Bud to overlook it or refrain from comment.

'I don't see anything to bark about,' Bud said with a puzzled look on his face. 'You've had a good job — in town ever' night. I thought when you got them powders that you'd go into deep mournin' and drop yo'r head like a mule colt with ticks in his ears.'

'I've tried it, and run up agin a hand that I couldn't play,' Bill said, and he lapsed into silence from which he refused to budge under Bud's further hints.

Bill's first thought was to wind up his official business. Long before the bank president, who was also secretary of the association, appeared at his office, Bill was sitting on the doorstep waiting. After a short conference he strode from the bank with a light step and hardly noticed the shamefaced Freddie Williams, who regarded him with an expression of mixed curiosity and apprehensiveness.

Back to the Tree Top with Bud West at his side rode Bill. The first part of the journey was marked by light-hearted joshing, but as the miles slipped away under the feet of their fast-traveling horses, Bill's lightness of heart became overshadowed by clouds of sorrow. He began to realize that he was throwing away the very thing that he wanted most, and that he had done the one thing above all other things that he did not want to do.

Once more Bill drowned his disappointment in hard work, and within two short days he announced to the Old Hoss that the herd was ready for travel. The second day after, they nooned and watered upon the Red Bank. As the herd climbed the long ridge toward Coleman Town Bill rode at the point, and a dull pain clutched at his heart when his gaze wandered to the little white schoolhouse, where it sat upon the low bench of ground two miles up the creek.

On through Coleman Town they went, and just as any other trail boss and his men would do, they bantered and badgered the two brand inspectors who combed through the herd for possible strays — Bud West being especially loud and boastful in offering wagers to any taker that no stray cattle would be found among them. Out along the base of the north-and-south hill range they went, following the deep worn trail made by countless thousands of cattle before them. Striking a course parallel to the hundredth meridian, they drove on north toward their far-away destination.

At the ranch, while Bill had been whipping the herd into shape, speculation was rife among the men as to what would become of Sancho. Some were confident that he would escape and never go over the trail. Bud West, whom Bill had selected to take charge of the first guard, made a bet of twenty dollars with some of the ranch hands that they would land the steer in Kansas. Hence he took steps at once to save the outfit from the embarrassment of losing Sancho, and incidentally to protect his twenty-dollar wager.

The first night out, he took his two partners into confidence and swore them to secrecy. At the fall of dark, one devoted his time to holding the herd, while the other two cut out Sancho and ran him to one side, where he was roped and tied securely to a tree for the night. Since it was their duty to relieve last guard early in the morning, the plot was completed when they threw Sancho to the ground and, after removing the rope from his neck, drove him back into the herd.

If Bill Sanders ever suspected anything from Sancho's gauntness and the rope marks around his neck, he kept his suspicions to himself, and the means of insuring the steer's presence each morning remained a mystery in spite of the amount of comment about his good behavior. After one week of the practice, Sancho became so accustomed to it that he learned to trot readily along and permit himself to be roped without making a wild run, and thus avoided the severe jerkings at the end of the race. He even no longer needed to be thrown in order to remove the rope next morning; he learned that it was less painful to stand quietly while one man rode up to his head and slipped the noose off. After the second week, Bud decided that the precaution was no longer necessary, and so it proved. Sancho was now displaying a surprising gentleness, and clung to the main body of the herd in a passive mood.

Sancho quickly adapted himself to the trail routine and appeared to like it. He at once asserted his leadership and took his place ahead. He seemed to enjoy the brisk walk in the cool of early morning after leaving the bed ground. Two hours of trailing and they would be thrown to one side and permitted to graze upon the abundant grass. After filling to capacity, they were allowed to trickle into the water and drink and then stretch out upon clean sand bars in the warm sun.

In mid-afternoon, Sancho would see Nig pulling out with his six-horse team for the night camp spot. This, he learned, was a signal for the cattle to move also. They were not put back on the trail and driven in the evening. Instead, they were allowed to scatter and graze along — guided and held in place by their drivers, who made it a point to see that every step taken was directed toward the far-away goal.

Lulled into sleep now were Sancho's old fear and hatred of men. He looked upon them as friendly and benevolent masters, and he worked himself into their esteem by his quick and ready response to their commands.

There were times, however, when his faith was strained almost to the breaking-point; times when the cowboys would squint knowingly at gathering thunderheads in the northwest, and bed rolls would be piled under an improvised shelter of canvas slung over a rope stretched tight between two trees. Nig would be seen tying down the wagon sheet securely around each end of the wagon box, and pulling it tight along the string of bows.

As night horses were saddled, slickers would be pulled from bed rolls and tied back of the cantle. Then, when the storm did break upon them with its fury of rolling thunder and zigzag lightning flashes, it was hard indeed for Sancho to retain his built-up confidence in his keepers, and allay his fears from the sound of their voices singing to him from the inky darkness.

There were other times when some of his more impetuous mates became alarmed and restless and started a stampede. In these times Sancho kept his self-control, and when the surge of running cattle would force him along, he made no attempt to escape. The progress they made was slow and tedious, but each step counted. The daily grind, as steady and relentless as a running stream, stretched out the miles behind them. Within a week they topped a high divide, and the long herd snaked its way down the slopes of the Brazos watershed and crossed over the river.

Then they moved over another plain and again dropped into rough breaks as they neared the Red River of Texas.

The muddy water rolled across a wide bottom, and carried an ominous threat to any one not familiar with the nature of the stream. Crossing the wagon was Bill's main concern, and after testing the depth on horseback he pronounced the stream fordable. He put four men to driving the *remuda* ahead of the wagon team as breakers. Two others, with ropes fastened to the rear axle of the wagon and their saddle-horns, rode slightly upstream and held the conveyance in line with the team.

When the wagon was across, the herd was started into the water, and Sancho trotted quickly into the lead. He reached the river bank, turned to his mates, and, bawling to them, drew a deep breath which swelled his sides and plunged in. The strong steer battled hard against the current. He found no swimming water, but it required steady walking to stand up in the shifting sand of the river bed. When his followers wavered in doubt and fear, he stopped and lent courage to them with his enticing bawl. He reached dry ground, and a line of wading cattle followed submissively, while men and floundering horses urged them ahead.

'That ox is wuth a thousand dollars,' commented Bud West. 'If I had him as a leader, I wouldn't be afraid to start a herd to Liverpool and swim the Atlantic Ocean.'

With the crossing of Red River, they passed from Texas soil into Indian Territory. Here they were often visited by small bands of Indians. They came as hungry beggars, and clung tenaciously behind the herd until Bill Sanders would relent and give them an animal to be butchered on the spot.

'And why?' asked one of Bud's guard companions, 'are we givin' beef to them lousy, greasy-haired Injuns?'

'It's a old custom,' whispered Bud. 'But I guess the fellers that started it had good reason. There was a time when a white man's scalp was a piece of personal property much coveted by Injuns. When the first herds started over the trail, some prudent boss insured his scalp by offerin' up a sacrifice of fresh beef. Next to a white man's scalp, Injuns liked beef. Other trail men followed suit and it soon got to be a practice. The Injuns have been sort of whipped out and they ain't dangerous any more — about the worst they do is to stampede a herd now and then and gather up some stragglers — but they think the beef gift ort to still be in effect.'

Bud slouched deeper in his saddle and pulled his hat brim sideways to shade his face from the evening sun. He swung his right leg across his horse's withers and patted the animal affectionately, while he peeped at the grazing cattle and watched Bill Sanders drive a lame steer out to the waiting Indians.

'Howbeit, as the Bible says,' drawled Bud, 'it can be said in the Injuns' favor that they aint a-tall choicy in their taste. Any kind of cow meat is cow meat to them, just like it is to a coyote. The trail men manage to confine their gifts of generosity to crippled, blind or otherwise ailin' animals that wouldn't git where they're goin' nohow, and wouldn't bring no money if they did. So it's still a satisfactory agreement all round.'

'Don't you worry none about yo'rself, Sancho, ol' boy,' Bill had said, as Sancho stood with head high and watched an Indian shoot down his less fortunate mate. 'The men in this outfit'd fight ever' Injun on the reservation to a stand still before they'd give up even that other horn of yours. They ain't no Injun ever goin' to flop a lip over any of yo'r beef. The steaks from yo'r carcass is bound for better things — such as to lay in big silver platters on long tables covered with white linen that's got tall glasses scattered over it filled with mint juleps and such.'

Steady driving across the Indian land brought them to where the Canadian River cut a deep scar across the face of high plains. The crest of dirty gray water with white-capped riffles from melting snowdrifts in the mountains rode high above the riverbed of quicksand. It spread from foothill to foothill nearly a half-mile apart, and Bill needed to make no test to measure the depth or gauge the current. He took one look at the heaving rolls and made his preparations for a long swim.

The place of crossing was known as Parker's Ford. The low buildings of a ranch lay close to the south bank of the river, and the ranch owner operated a ferryboat during the flood season. Therefore, Bill sought out the rancher and made arrangements for crossing his wagon on the ferry next morning.

At the break of dawn, the wagon was ferried across. Then the herd was strung out into trailing line and pointed toward the river.

Sancho was taken from his place in the lead and held in reserve. Bill had Meletone and two other men throw the *remuda* into the lead, and used them as a toll to get the cattle into the water. The swift current hurled the leaders downstream so fast that the line broke, and only a few hundred animals were crossed at the first trial. The saddle-horses were crossed and recrossed, until they refused to enter the water without strong urging. It was then that Bill ordered Sancho put in his proper place.

When the herd was re-formed and started, Sancho made his way to the water, turned, and bawled to his mates and plunged in. Before he was halfway across, the line broke in two and left three hundred timid cattle upon the south bank. Urgent pressure failed to move them into the water, and then Bud West hit upon a scheme for employing Sancho again.

He communicated his idea to Bob Long, and after a lengthy discussion they laid it before Bill Sanders and the ferryman.

'We'll cut down some of them cottonwood trees and make a corral on the ferry,' explained Bud. 'Then we'll poll over and ferry ol' Sancho back to this side.'

'You couldn't drag Sancho onto that ferry with a steam engine,' snorted Dave Houston. 'And if you did, he wouldn't stay there as long as I could hold a wild hoss by the tail.'

'I'll bet ten dollars we can,' Bud retorted. 'We'll take the ferryman's four milk cows over and drive 'em close to the herd. Then we'll cut out Sancho and mix 'im with the gentle cows and he'll follow 'em right onto that boat. One of us can ride back to make things sort of steady.'

'Yeah,' Dave sneered. 'I don't want to be the one. Ol' Sancho's liable to upset the whole outfit in the middle of the river and dump it into the water. I don't mind a little swim, but I don't want to git tangled up with a ferryboat and a lot of poles when I do it.'

'I never heerd of such a thing,' said the ferryman, pulling upon an old black pipe. 'But I live and learn, and I'll try anything once.'

Bill assented to the scheme and took the lead. He rode on board the ferry and told the boatman to push off. It took much coaxing to work Sancho onto the boat with the gentle cows, but at last he came along. While in midstream, he threatened to wreck things as he set himself for a wild jump into the bars of the frail corral, but Bill's soothing words eased his fears and he made the trip without incident.

After Sancho had led the remaining cattle into midstream, a large tree came drifting at them. Its widespread branches were riding foremost and half submerged. It floated into the swimming cattle and threw them into a wild panic. They milled around together in a confused huddle and washed downstream. Bill Sanders swam his horse into the mixup and tried to break the mill. The tree jammed into him and trapped the horse in its branches. The animal floundered and went down among the jam of struggling cattle.

Bill was pulled from his horse by the current. As he was sinking, he grasped a limb of the tree, which snapped off in his hand. The horse broke surface just out of his reach and swam ashore. Dave Houston plunged into the pack of swimming animals and flung the coils of his rope at the sinking man. The rope lodged on a tree branch, and before he could gather it up and make another throw, Bill went out of sight.

The heavy silt of fine sand which kept afloat while churning around in the current was settling inside Bill's clothes and pulling him under with its dead weight. While he struggled against the current, he saw the white face of Sancho bearing down upon him. The steer's sides bulged like the expanding chambers of a bellows, and the air whistled back and forth through his distended nostrils.

Bill flounced to one side and dodged the rush, but as Sancho swam by he threw an arm around the steer's neck. The force of his speed against the current swung Bill's body alongside, and he scrambled to Sancho's back. Finally, at a place where the long-legged steer could find bottom, Bill was bucked off in the water. This time Dave Houston's rope did not miss its mark, and the half-drowned cowboy was towed safely to shore.

Bill replaced his sand-laden clothes with dry ones, and expressed himself as feeling fine after the bath, but the experience left him in a sobered mood. While the other men were straightening out the camp and making ready for the next day's drive, he rode out and stayed with the herd until darkness. He rode around to where Sancho was grazing, and leaning forward and resting his chin in his upturned hand, Bill looked for a long time at the grazing steer.

'It looks like me and you are tied together now, ol' feller,' he said. 'If I just had you back on the Tree Top, I'd set you free.'

CHAPTER SEVENTEEN
SHIPPIN' OUT TO MONTANA

THREE weeks later, Bill stopped his outfit on the Arkansas, six miles above the wild cow town of Dodge City, Kansas. The countryside was dotted with other herds, awaiting sales or room in the busy railroad yards, where crews of men worked day and night loading cattle for shipment to Kansas City and Chicago for slaughter, or into the corn belt for finishing.

'Bill hates to leave ol' Sancho,' confided Bud West to the balance of the camp that evening. 'The closer we git to the end of the trail, the jollier all of us are — but Bill. He sort of acts like he was goin' to see a dead brother.'

'That ain't what's the matter with Bill,' disputed Dave Houston. 'He's got gal trouble.'

'You ort to know what that feels like,' retorted Bud. 'You've been there yo'rself.'

Bud fished a coal from the fire and lit his cigarette. He puffed awhile in silence, and then turned to Dave Houston.

'They's somethin' wrong about Bill and his gal, all right — but that's all his business.'

At Six Mile Camp, the Old Hoss met them with a prospective buyer, whom he introduced to Bill and the outfit as a Mr. Collins. He was not, the buyer explained, a market speculator, nor an Eastern feeder. He was a range man, just as they were, and he was manager of a syndicate in Montana and they were now stocking up with fifty thousand steers. He had heard of the good breeding of the Tree Top cattle and the well-trained cow ponies, and he would try to buy the outfit.

The deal was quickly closed. There was no jockeying for advantage, no price haggling. Bill felt a little thrill of admiration as those two rugged business men faced each other in frankness and made a trade amounting to more than fifty thousand dollars. A price was asked, an offer made and accepted. Before Bill could realize what had been done, the entire outfit had been sold, in range vernacular, 'horn, hide, and hoof,' meaning, the cattle, horses, wagon and all equipment, and the services of the men if they were willing to go.

Bill drew a heavy sigh of relief when an opportunity opened up for him to remove himself further from his sad disappointment. But a majority of the men were not inclined to obligate themselves without argument.

'You ain't talkin' to me, mister,' demurred Bob Long. 'I know a few fellers that went to that country, but they all come back. They say it gits cold enough there to freeze the horns off a billy goat or the nose offen a wooden Injun.'

'You're wrong there,' denied Collins. 'It gets cold all right, but it's not as bad as you think. Texas men and Texas cattle stand the winters just as well as natives. Besides, Montana is the coming cattle country. It'll be a long time before the nesters run the cowmen out like they're doing further south. The wages are good, and just to show you I mean what I say, I'll double the pay of every man.'

Bill Sanders had sat quietly during the conversation. He wanted his men with him. He knew that grave responsibilities were in store for the man that drove a herd all the way to Montana over unknown country. He slid from his seat and stood up. He looked out over the herd and spotted Sancho leading the way to water.

'Let's all go, fellers,' he said. 'There ain't been a quitter yet
that rode the Tree Top ponies, and I'd hate to think there's a man
in this outfit that cain't stand the gaff.'

Bud West uncrossed his legs and threw one foot forward
and dug his spur rowel into the ground. The rowel whizzed on
its rivet as he jerked his feet under and stood up. A grin played
around the corners of his mouth, and walking to Bill's side he
grasped him by the arm.

'I'm with you, pardner, till hell freezes over,' he said.

Bob Long sprang up and took his place beside the two men.
'And when you fellers git there,' he said, 'you'll find me skatin'
right along by yo'r warm side.'

'Me too' — 'Me too,' burst suddenly from all the other men
but Nig, who stood silently poking at the fire.

'You think a niggah'll be safe in dthat cold no'then cuentry,
mistah Bill?'

"Course you'll be safe,' interrupted Bud West. 'This whole
outfit is behind you stronger'n hoss radish ; and I'd like to see the
color of the man's eye that'd dare harm a single hair on that ol'
black head of yo'rn.'

'Whahevah you all go—I go too,' he beamed proudly, and a
twinkle came into his dark eyes.

'Good!' exclaimed Collins. 'That's all settled now. You fellows excuse me and Bill while we get our heads together and map
out the drive.'

Drawing Bill aside, Collins sat down, facing the north. He
brushed a smooth place in the dirt in front of him and picking up
a small stick, placed the end of it near the left toe of his crossed
legs.

'This is where we are now; and over there,' he said, moving
the stick a short distance from him, 'is Fort Hays on the K.P.
Railroad. It's about seventy-five miles, and when you get there
you can ship out through Denver and Cheyenne to the head
of the Powder River in Wyoming. That will cut off six or seven

hundred miles of trail and get the steers on the range and settled before winter.'

Collins then moved the point of his stick to his left, and away from him in the general direction of the northwest. 'This is where you unload,' he said. Then he drew a line straight to the north and crossed it with another running at right angles. 'This,' he said, indicating the first line, 'is the way the Powder runs. And this is where you will cross the Yellowstone after driving down the Powder to its mouth. Then, you'll be about fifty miles from the divide of the Yellowstone and Missouri Rivers. I'll have a man meet you there and pilot you to the divide. You can make a turn-loose and come on to the Buzzard X Ranch. I will be there.'

Collins then smoothed out the lines he had traced. Drawing a figure of a large X with wings standing out from the upper points, he said: 'That's the Buzzard X brand. You'll have to put it on these steers. There's a good branding chute and corrals in the Fort Hays stockyards, and that is the best place to brand.'

He reached into his coat pocket and pulled out a checkbook and handed it to Bill. 'Just sign "The Northwest Cattle Company by William Sanders" to the checks for expenses. The local banks and trading posts along the trail will honor them the same as they do in your country. The railroad might not want to take your check for the freight, so I'll have our bank wire guarantee of payment. Then there won't be any hitch about unloading when you get into Wyoming.'

'That,' he said, 'is all. If anything else comes up, just use your own judgment. Good luck, and I hope to see you in six weeks or two months,' he finished standing up and shaking Bill's hand.

'Good-bye, Bill,' said the Old Hoss. 'When the smoke all clears away and this herd is delivered, I'm looking for you back at the Tree Top.'

'I'll be there,' replied Bill; but he knew better. He could see another life opening before him where he hoped to forget the past.

Next morning, Bill pointed the herd to the north. Six days later, he pitched camp on the banks of the Smokey, near Fort Hays. While unrolling his bed, he heard the approach of horses and heard Bud West inviting some one to dismount and share the comforts of camp.

'I want to see the boss first,' came a reply in a rasping voice that had a familiar sound.

'Aw, git down,' scoffed Bud. 'This ain't no tightwad outfit. You don't have to git permission from our boss to eat.'

As Bill turned around the wagon, he saw three saddle horses and another, laden with a pack. One of the horses was a snuff-colored brown that tossed his head and rolled a pair of prominent flashing eyes. In the dim light of the campfire, Bill recognized the flaming beard and shifting eyes of Ben Harte. At his side stood Jack Barnes and the lanky Mexican Juan, with his drooping mustache and shaggy brows.

'What're you doin' here?' asked Bill tersely.

'I heard you was shippin' out to Montana, and we'd like to throw in with you an' go along,' replied Harte.

Bill eyed him for an instant and then replied: 'You've got yo'r gall. It looks like you'd know by this time that I ain't in the habit of throwin' in with cow thieves.'

Harte dropped his shifting gaze before the calm stare of Bill and then he laughed softly and without bitterness.

'I know you ain't got no use for me,' he replied, 'but I didn't think you was the kind to shove a drownin' man under the water. I've hit it hard the last two or three years, and I've sort of decided to change my ways. I've learnt I cain't buck the game agin the law — so I've give up and aim to try fer somethin' else.' Harte was peering at Bill expectantly out of narrow-slitted eyes; Barnes was exploring the ground at his feet, and the Mexican Juan was looking at the stars.

'What're you leavin' the country in such a hurry for now?' Bill asked.

'It's this way,' explained Harte with a ring of downcast sincerity in his voice. 'The run-in I had with the law a few years ago broke me up in business and I couldn't never git started agin. Last winter the bank took over all I had left but a little herd that I drove up this spring behind you. Them hosses there,' he said with a slight sweep of his hand at the three saddled ponies and the pack animal, 'is all I've got out of them fine Arabian ponies. Me and Jack and Juan here is on our way to Montana to start all over agin.'

'— and start stealin' soon's you git there,' finished Bill.

'No, si-ree!' denied Harte. 'I swear that if you'll give us a lift and help us — I'll never steal another cow — or cross yo'r trail as long's I live.'

While Bill stood with indecision, he let his eye run over the four horses showing fatigue from a long ride. He stepped over and laid his arm affectionately upon the *grullo's* neck and patted him.

'You fellers unsaddle and stay all night,' he said, turning away from the horse. 'We've got to brand out this herd tomorrow. Durin' that time, I'll study about givin' you a lift. If you want to part with that pony,' Bill said, again turning his admiring gaze upon the *grullo,* 'I'll dig up a hundred dollars for 'im right now.'

'I couldn't sell,' replied Harte, affecting a sorrowful tone. 'He's all I've got left.'

'I don't know's if I blame you,' replied Bill with the first indication of warmth in his voice during the interview. 'If that hoss was mine, it'd take more'n a thousand dollars to jar me loose from 'im.'

At the break of dawn, Sancho was among the first five hundred cattle to be cut off from the main bunch and driven into the stockyards. He had a premonition that all was not well when he sniffed at the smoke from the fire outside. He knew that he had got himself into a trap when he was swept into the narrow confines of a branding chute ahead of a wave of fear-crazed animals, endeavoring to escape from the threats of yipping voices and rattling cans. Then came the final knowledge when Bob Long straddled the chute wall with a red-hot branding iron in his hand and burned the ✕ into his side, just back of the old Tree Top.

Harte and his companion threw themselves into the branding with unstinted zeal. Upon every turn it appeared that one of them was in the right place at the right time. Bill watched this display of skillful knowledge, and during the day a struggle was going on within him between his dislike for a thief and his admiration for a good cowhand. At last the feeling of cowboy fellowship won out and Harte was permitted to accompany the outfit.

CHAPTER EIGHTEEN

'WE'RE LOOKIN' FER A GANG OF BANK ROBBERS'

ONE hard day was to follow another. The two thousand steers with their fresh brand of the Buzzard X were started again into the stockyards at daylight. A locomotive towing a long string of freight cars slid into the station and came to a stop. Very soon, fresh-branded steers were being crowded up the runway of the loading chute into the cars — all as a result of a conference between Bill and the train dispatcher.

It required three full trains to move the outfit. Four cars were provided with hay for the horses. A box car was furnished for the wagon and camp equipment. In this car Nig set up his contraptions and was soon serving products of his excellent culinary skill. Bill Sanders, with three cars of horses, the chuck car, and most of the men, departed on the first train.

Three hundred miles of sun-bleached plains were traversed with the dust sucking up from the ground and mingling with engine smoke of the speeding trains. Next morning found them in the cooler altitudes of the Rocky Mountain foothills. At Denver the cars were switched to the stockyards and unloaded for a short rest and feed and water. Here, the outfit was reunited

But the last train had no more than arrived and unloaded when the first one was again on its way. Flanking the mountain foothills, the train wound its way on a steady climb to the high plains of Wyoming. Upon the third day after loading at Fort Hays, the cars were set to a blind siding high upon the headwaters of Powder River in Wyoming.

Sancho reeled as he walked down the unloading chute with the other half-starved and exhausted animals. They entered into a mad scramble to reach the choicest water and grass, and as a result Bill Sanders, Harte, and the other men had their hands full in quieting them down.

At the first opportunity, Harte and his men held a whispered consultation and immediately started their preparations to leave the outfit. While they were saddling, Bill approached them.

'You're a good cowman, Ben — as good as ever come out of the brush in Southern Texas,' he said. 'If you aim to go straight like you said — I think I can get you a job with this outfit.'

Harte pulled his cinch strap tighter and the *grullo* horse winced under the pain. He tossed the lead rope of the pack horse to the Mexican Juan, who was already mounted. He stepped lightly into his stirrup and turned to Bill.

'I ain't huntin' fer no job,' he said brusquely, 'and if anybody asks you where we went to you can say you don't know, fer you don't.'

With that they rode away, and Bill watched them disappear through a low gap in the hills to the northwest.

The other trains were arriving, and Bill was kept busy with the nervous cattle. While alone on the back side of the herd, he was approached by five strange men, all heavily armed.

'Whut outfit's this?' asked the leader in a gruff voice.

'The Tree Top,' Bill replied, 'but we've been sold to the Buzzard X and we're on our way into Montana.'

''T's whut I thought,' grunted the other. He then turned and said something aside to his followers.

Bill saw the men scatter around him, and he noted that their hands were significantly near the handles of their pistols. One had drawn his rifle from its scabbard and sat with it resting across the bow of his saddle. Instinctively Bill's right hand came down near the butt of his own gun.

'Don't do it, pard,' warned the leader. 'They's five of us and one of you. We've got you covered, and if you start to draw that hog-leg — it'll be yo'r own mistake.'

Bill's deep frown at the men faded into a wide grin.

'Shore. You can cut me in two — but what then?' he smiled. 'Don't you see them other men with this outfit? How long do you think you'd last?'

'Just stand hitched — and answer a few questions,' interposed the leader, 'and you'll be all right. We're officers — savvy? And we'd like to look yo'r outfit over. Whut's them hosses branded?'

Bill drew a deep breath and settled easily into his saddle.

'You've got a funny way to approach a man,' he said. 'But you're wastin' time to hunt stolen hosses in this outfit. They're all branded the Tree Top and ain't got another scratch on 'em. You can look till you go blind if you want to.'

'We ain't exactly after stole hosses,' replied the posse leader.

'All right,' said Bill. 'You can turn this outfit upside down if you want to. There's nothin' wrong with any of us — I've knowed every man for——' Bill hesitated. He looked through the gap in the hills and then faced the possemen.

'If you'll tell me what you want, I might save time for you.'

The posse leader held a short consultation with one of his men, and then fished into his pocket and brought forth a yellow slip of paper.

'We're lookin' fer a gang of bank robbers. The sheriff down at Dodge City, Kansas, sent us this tel-ee-gram that they was some fellers helt up a bank and that they was headed this way. I fig-gered they'd jine up with some cow outfit.'

Bill glanced again at the low gap in the hills to the northwest.

'Seems to me like you've made a good guess, officer. What's them fellers' names and what do they look like?'

The posse leader scanned the slip of paper again and spelled out the words in a mumbling voice.

'This hyar don't say nothin' about whut their names is, but they's supposed to be two white fellers and a Mex'kin. They're ridin' hosses branded the deuce o' hearts and one hoss is a *grullo*. Whut the hell is a *grullo* anyhow?' he drawled slowly, squirting a stream of tobacco juice between his horse's ears.

Bill grinned — grinned until he almost laughed out loud — in spite of the knowledge that Harte's bad-luck story had fooled him.

'I guess the drinks are on me this time, pardner. You're on the right track — but you're a little slow. The fellers you're after rode through that gap in the hills about three hours ago. And *grullo*,' he continued, 'is the Mexican name for a snuff-colored brown hoss and it's pronounced *Grew-yo*.'

Bill looked at the heavy-boned, thick-bodied horses of the possemen and mentally compared them with the wiry, clean-limbed, Arabian-blooded mounts of Harte and his two followers.

'Pardner,' he said, 'I ain't tryin' to throw cold water on yo'r hopes, but I believe you'd just as well turn back and not grieve any over spilt milk. There ain't no more chance of you catchin' up with them deuce of hearts ponies than there is of me preachin' a sermon in the village church-house. You might meet them fellers comin' back some day — but I'll swear you'll never overtake 'em on them movin' mountains of hossflesh that you're ridin'.'

The posse leader spat another stream to the ground and yawned. 'Wal, all right. Don't know's I care much nohow, 'long's they git out o' the country. With all these hyar trail herds a-movin' we've got about all we can take keer of right hyar to home.'

CHAPTER NINETEEN
"GOOD-BYE, SANCHO"

AFTER a day's rest on feed and water, the herd was swung into shape and pointed down the Powder on the final leg of the long journey. As they moved along, a strange and picturesque topography greeted the view of Bill Sanders and his men. It was not like the rugged hills of Texas with its covering of thorny brush, nor like the high, treeless plains of western Kansas. Instead, the low banks of the river gave way to a flat valley bottom covered with a growth of scrubby sage, interwoven by tall stems of rank grama grass. The wide valleys butted squarely against choppy badlands of clay and chalk compositions, glittering in the sunlight with thickly strewn flakes of mica. The badland buttes and bluffs appeared to serve as footstools for the towering peaks and ridges, which stacked upon each other in gigantic sections until, far back and high up, their heavy fringe of pine-tree covering blended with the deep blue of the skyline.

'Keep 'em drillin' along,' were the orders Bill now passed out. 'We're drivin' to range and grass instead of to market, and it won't hurt none if they are a little ga'nted up when we git there.' Thus, the sleepy loungings around watering places were at an end. With only enough time out for grazing to insure traveling strength, the long herd crawled steadily toward the end of the drive.

The nights were developing a sharp chill, and a coating of frost glittered in brilliant sparkles against the morning sun rays. During their guard periods, the men shivered in their clothing, suitable for Texas weather but sadly out of place in Montana. Their supply of bedding was noticeably scant, and Bill Sanders expressed their plight when he remarked to a visitor at the camp one day:

'The boys've dug down in their sugans a quilt deeper at a time ever' few nights till they've dug into the ground.'

On they drove, without stop or let up. Nig's wagon wheels were now turning most of the day, testing his ingenuity to keep out in front of that ever-moving string of cattle, with long-legged Sancho swinging ahead and setting the pace. On they drove, day by day watching a blurred rim ahead slowly raising into distinct outlines of towering bluffs and Bad Land peaks which Bill had been told lined the north bank of the mighty Yellowstone River.

The men were now hearing from almost every camp visitor about the dangers of swimming the Yellowstone.

'There ain't no use'n you tryin' to pick a load into this outfit, pardner,' Bud West would invariably reply. 'You ain't seen nothin' yet. Jus' foller us down to yo'r little river. Ol' Sancho'll hit it full in the face and bust it wide open like a ripe watermelon.'

Fortunately they reached the much-talked-of stream at the most desirable time in the year for crossing. Back in the high altitudes of the Rockies where water from melting snowdrifts trickles away and gathers into the main body of the river, freezing temperatures were already checking the flow. Therefore, with the water at its low mark and not yet too cold for swimming, they crossed with hardly a ripple in their schedule. Working in the lead, Sancho waded as far as possible, and then struck his swimming stride. Showing confidence in his leadership, his mates followed closely, and without breaking the line in two the entire herd reached the north bank.

Beyond the Yellowstone, they were met by a man riding a horse branded Buzzard X on the left hip. He had been sent, he said, by Cliff Collins, to pilot them onto the range. Following the stranger's direction Bill pointed the herd, and upon the seventh of September Sancho led the way over the pine-studded divide which separates the Missouri and Yellowstone Rivers.

As the lead cattle turned down the north slope, Bill rode in front and slowed their advance, spreading them out fanwise behind him. Other men topped the divide, and they joined Bill and helped him check the moving cattle. Bill had been correct in his statement that morning when he said it was easy to get a string of cattle moving but not so easy to get them stopped. From habit formed by months on the trail, the steers were reluctant to separate and go their individual ways again. Thus, for a half-day Bill and his men were busy, working gently, spreading the herd out on the new range.

Bill rode to the top of a low hill, and by signal conveyed an order to his men to ride away and leave the cattle alone. He watched Sancho disappear into a cluster of willow trees down a draw.

'Good-bye, Sancho, old boy,' he said, more to himself than to anyone else. 'I wish you good luck and a full life for a steer. I guess I've seen you my last time.'

There was silence and an air of misgiving among the cowboys who gathered around the man who had directed them over the two thousand miles of trail that separated them from Texas soil. Bill could read in their faces the knowledge that this day marked the end of their association as a body of men. Each one seemed to know that the time had come when he must part company with his string of saddle horses; the horses that had borne him faithfully day and night — over good ground and bad — across raging streams and desert land. And still, they knew nothing of Bill's secret determination to stay away from Texas.

'It's about time for chuck,' reminded the Buzzard X man. 'I camped yo'r wagon at the ranch,' he continued, pointing to a group of low buildings a mile further down the creek.

'Hell, yes!' exploded Bud West. 'Let's go eat, drink or do somethin'. You fellers'll have me cryin' in a minute. You look like a bed of pansies after frost falls.'

At the camp, Collins came to offer gratulations for their successful trip. He instructed Bill to draw checks payable to each man for his time and add enough for their transportation back to Texas. Then he offered a job to any or all that cared to stay in Montana.

Nig was the first to speak. 'Nunh. Unh! mistah boss. Ise already drifted fah afield. I'se gwine a see dthat black gal o' mine down whah dthem cotton blossoms grow, or bust a hoof. No sah ! mistah boss. You ain't said nothin' yit to hold dthis niggah. I's shivahed my last shivah!'

'That's the ticket, Nig,' approved Dave Houston. 'You've said a mouthful for all of us. I aim to hit that trail for Texas full in the face.'

Bill Sanders was sitting on a bed roll, with his own thoughts far away. He was sadly recalling the time when a girl had turned from him with words of rebuke and walked away with another man — recently sobered. He arose and walked into the crowd of noisy cowboys and faced the general manager.

'If you've got a place for me, I think I'll stay,' he said simply.

A sudden hush fell over the group, and mouths gaped open at Bill's announcement. Dave Houston was the first to gain speech.

'You don't want to stay in this God-forsaken country, Bill,' he sputtered. 'You're just mad — you just ——' and his voice trailed to indistinct mumbling at a threatening gleam in Bud West's eye. 'You just hate to leave ol' Sancho,' Dave finished.

'What's it to you if Bill does hate to leave ol' Sancho?' challenged Bud. 'And I'm goin' to stay with 'im too. What'd'y think o' that?'

'I don't give a damn what you do,' retorted Dave. 'But if Bill stays up here, I think he's crazy.'

'Yeah,' snarled Bud. 'But he ain't crazy over a gal that'd have her looks improved if she wore her pap's whiskers——'

'I've told you once!' shouted Dave, lunging forward and striking Bud in the face. Before Bill could reach them, they were fighting.

'Let 'em fight!' yelled Bob Long, jumping forward and grasping Bill. 'They've had their necks bowed like a couple of mad bulls for the last two years——'

'Not now. Not now,' Bill said firmly, shaking Bob loose. 'They're about to part, and they're goin' to shake hands like men.'

The two cowboys glared at each other.

'Don't you peep a word about Bill's gal; if you do, I'll beat yo'r gizzard out,' hissed Bud West.

'And the same goes to you about my gal,' whispered Dave as their hands fell apart from the forced handshake.

A large, white-topped spring wagon pulled by four prancing horses drew up at the camp. The driver jumped to the ground and wrapped his lines around the brake staff.

'All abo-o-o-r-d,' he called. 'If you miss this rig you'll have to walk. All aboard for Beaverpond, Kansas City, Fote Wuth, and all Texas points. Shake a leg, cowboys. We've just got time to catch the eight o'clock train out of Beaverpond.'

While bedding, saddles, and other personal belongings were being stowed into the luggage rack, Nig turned to Bill with tears streaming down his cheeks.

'Good-bye, mistah Bill,' he sobbed. 'I hates to leave you all in dthis heah col' ceuntry. You mus' remembah theah'll always be a fiah o' welcome buhnin' foh you in dthe Tree Top kitchen.'

Bill was forced to turn away to hide his own emotion. There stood the faithful Nig, the silent Meletone, looking at him reproachfully. 'Good-bye,' he said shaking hands with them both. 'I'll be back to see you some day.'

'Shore!' agreed Bud West. 'Me and Bill will make our stakes an' come back some time with our pockets full of spondulicks. I think I'd cry too if I knowed I was goin' back to a country where cow grass is being dug up for cotton and a cowhand is goin' to have to strap a sack on his back and go down between two rows, snatchin' lint with both hands to make a livin'.'

CHAPTER TWENTY

THE STORM

WHEN winter set in, Bill Sanders and Bud West were assigned to a line camp, forty miles from the home ranch, on the high divide between the Missouri and Yellowstone Rivers. It was their duty to ride line along the divide and throw all drifting Buzzard X cattle back north toward the Missouri. After freezing weather set in, they had to chop ice and keep drinking places in water holes open along the divide.

A single-room log house had been erected for their camp, and a small shed joined to the house as shelter for their horses during the coldest weather. Immediately back of the shed room was a lot, enclosing a stack of hay.

As the two men rounded the corner of their horse-shed one morning in November, the sing of stretching wire and crash of breaking fence posts greeted their ears. They hurried around to see a large, onehorned steer break from the enclosure, carrying a section of the stack lot fence across his neck and shoulders.

'I'll be damned!' exclaimed Bill. 'Sancho, you ol' scalawag. You're up to yo'r tricks again. I'm glad to see you, ol' boy, but we've got to draw the line right now. This little dab o' hay is all we've got to run our ponies this winter, and we cain't spare any of it.'

'Now, Bill,' chided Bud West as they put the finishing touches of repair to the stack lot fence, 'You might make some fellers swallow that talk, but you cain't fool me none. You drove ol' Sancho up here last night when you come in, and you stole out a fork of hay and fed it to 'im too.'

Sancho never found means to overcome the added reinforcement to the fence, but he still hung around the camp. Many times the hungry look in his begging eyes caused Bill to elude Bud and sneak from the cabin and recklessly throw the steer a fork of precious hay under cover of darkness.

As the season turned on the equinox hub and the sun started its slow climb toward its summer orbit, men and animals alike waited in hopeful expectancy. Would the winter show the first signs of break soon, and great ice floes go thundering down river gorges in an early thaw, or would the weather tighten and drag along into a late spring? These were the thoughts paramount in Bill's mind as he watched closely for a change in nature's barometer. And upon a thick day in January, when an invisible haze dimmed the sun's luster, the peculiar actions of the cattle did not escape him.

'We're goin' to have a blowout, and a ring-tailed one at that,' he prophesied, resting the blade of his axe on the ground and watching the cattle drink from recently opened holes. 'Jus' look at the way them cattle is drinkin'. They've already had one fill today and now they're comin' for more. Look at ol' Sancho. He's swelled like a toad and his water tank is about to bust wide open.'

Bud raised his face and peered at the horizon rim. 'I cain't see no signs of a storm,' he said.

'I cain't see no storm sign neither,' Bill agreed. 'But them cattle see it. Their instinct has done told 'em. They know that before another time to water rolls around, they'll have their tails tucked between their legs and driftin' from a cold wind.'

'Good-bye, Sancho,' Bill called in farewell, when the large steer scrambled awkwardly up a bank and moved away with his sides bulging from the reserve water in his stomach. 'Adios, and good luck,' Bill called again.

Before bedtime, a wall of dark clouds floated up and rimmed the northwestern horizon. By midnight a fresh breath of wind was stirring among the pine leaves, and depositing scattered pellets of snow. The crack of breaking fibre awoke Bill when the frozen tree limbs bent into a swaying motion before a stiff breeze. He lay awake and listened, and heard the breeze change from a low whistle to a wailing roar. One blast of wind overtook another into a terrific gale which shrieked and howled around the projecting eaves and ridgepoles of the log cabin.

The two line riders were out at daylight. Sharp pellets of driven ice cut into the exposed parts of their numbed faces. A biting chill crept up from fingertips and found its way under heavy clothing to their bodies. Downy frost collected upon horses' manes and ear tips, and icicles from their hot breath clung to nostrils as they struggled through banked snowdrifts.

An hour of riding and exposure to the bitter cold convinced the men that their efforts to stem the tide of drifting cattle were futile. Every low dip in the divide ridge held a string of animals which refused to turn around and face the storm.

'Might as well try to stop the Yellowstone with a broom,' yelled Bill above the wind. 'We'll hit for camp and stay indoors till she blows over.'

Sancho fought the storm. He lowered his head, while he bucked against the gale and refused to join the waves of his mates that were flowing across the divide, but he sought shelter close at hand. He made his way to the line camp, sidling against the bitter wind, by dead instinct, and stopped in the L corner of the stable and cabin.

He was protected from the wind, but deep snow drifted around him. Before daylight, the growing snow bed had built halfway up his sides. The bitter cold clutched at his shivering body and drove him out to seek warmth through exercise, and he turned over the divide into a draw leading south.

He drifted along to where a solid floor of ice bridged the Yellowstone from bank to bank. Sancho crossed over and headed up the winding trails of the Powder, by which he had entered the country six months before.

All sense of direction departed from him. All thoughts of the future were lacking. Only the instinct of self-preservation drove him on before the biting wind. His legs throbbed with a numbed ache, and exhaustion pulled heavily at him. The sharp edges of frozen ground rasped the bottoms of his feet into raw tenderness, but a fighting heart kept him moving. Frozen carcasses strewn along the trail told him what happened to animals that stopped to rest. Mountainous snowdrifts arose in his pathway, but his reserve strength carried him on. Many times he was forced to leave the broken trail to plow his way around some weaker animal that had succumbed to the strain and cold.

Darkness followed daylight over and over again, with only intermittent lulls to break the deadly monotony. Through frost-stained windows of their log cabin the line riders saw cattle drifting by, with brands that placed their homes north of the Missouri. All of them showed a gauntness from enforced travel and lack of food. Some walked with the sturdy precision of strong animals, while others reeled by on bleeding feet, precluding an early death in a snow-bank.

'There'll be one grand round-up if spring ever does come,' prophesied Bill. 'I wish Banjy could see this drift. He's seen ever'thing, but I'll bet he never seen anything like this.'

'If this keeps up,' hazarded Bud, 'there won't be enough cattle left to make a round-up.'

'There'll be a lot of 'em die,' admitted Bill, 'but there'll be a lot of 'em left alive. There'll be enough work here next spring to keep ever' cowhand in Montana ridin' like a drunk Injun all summer to straighten out the mix-up.'

As suddenly as it had begun, the storm ended. The north wind died at sundown with lingering stubbornness, and the cold reached its brittle climax during the night with temperatures dropping far below zero. Next morning, while the sun flashed over banks of sparkling snow, a gentle chinook wind puffed up from the southwest. The sun climbed higher, the wind increased in velocity, and the snowdrifts started shrinking before its warm blasts. As the wind sliced tops from snowcapped mounds, carcasses of frozen cattle appeared above the white level and told a mute story of the appalling loss in livestock.

Sancho paused in his forced journey, seventy-five miles from home. He ate his first grass when it was slowly uncovered from the snow, and he drank his first water as it gathered in little puddles from melting drifts. For the first time during the long week he found a bed of dry grass and sagebrush to lie upon and rest his aching legs and smarting feet.

From the grim, weather-beaten men of the widely scattered line camps over the land there came trickling information of the gigantic shift of cattle from the home ranges. The cattle barons assembled, weighed this information, and called a joint meeting for early spring. In the middle of April, hundreds of men and thousands of saddle horses, representing thirty cow outfits, gathered in and around the town of Beaver-pond. At this meeting, plans were agreed upon to work the entire country and relocate a confused and wandering mixture of cattle which were now scattered over parts of three states.

Acting under advice of experienced range bosses, the cattle magnates decided to form a line with their round-up wagons, far to the south in Wyoming, and work back in unison, breasting through a tract of country more than three hundred miles wide. And for the first time in the history of the Montana cattle country, range outfits from the north side pulled their wagons south of the Yellowstone.

Bill Sanders was silent under the weight of his responsibilities. He was to lead the Buzzard X forces and form the spearhead of the whole drive. He took pride at the thought of coming in charge of the largest single range working outfit he had ever seen put together. Two hundred and fifty head of saddle horses swelled his *remuda* until it compared in size to a moderate trail herd itself. Two large wagons, drawn by heavy-boned, six-horse teams were required for provision, bedding, corral ropes, and other camp paraphernalia. And coming under Bill's direct authority were twenty-five cowboys, three wranglers, and a cook.

Thus, mounted once more on a string of his old Tree Top cow ponies, Bill led his outfit up the Powder to the Wyoming line. Here, on the twenty-fifth of April, he swung around. Upon this day, the big push started, and sun-tanned men rode circle from dawn till darkness, sweeping over a line of country from the Big Horn to the Little Missouri.

Bill often wondered about the fate of Sancho. Now, as his outfit gradually worked back toward home and his herd of Buzzard X cattle grew in size by hundreds, he began to fear the worst for the old steer. He made close observation of all carcasses of dead animals that he came across and he asked his men to do the same. But ten days after starting his drive, he was relieved from anxiety. Sancho came plunging into the round-up, as lively as ever, and fully recovered from the privations of the blizzard.

Bill worked his way northward until he reached the Yellowstone during the last part of May. The river was now at highest flood stage. The current boiled and heaved from its load of foam-capped water, and whirlpools went spinning swiftly along with the flow. Bill formed his monstrous herd into line back from the river and started. Once more the veteran cowboy's heart swelled with pride as he watched his old pet — the steer to which he owed so much — inflate his sides like a balloon, and without hesitation plunge into the roaring current and lead the hesitating cattle to the north shore.

Sancho settled upon the range, and his first summer was a thriving one. In all his life he had never been blessed with such an abundance of feed. The blacktopped grama and buffalo grasses were growing in wasteful profusion wherever he roamed. For once, his greedy appetite met its match and he gorged himself into uncomfortable fullness. His large paunch stretched to such proportions that it crowded his lung space, and his breath came in short, labored puffs as he rested upon his haunches and chewed his cud.

That fall, the Buzzard X started shipping their first beef to market. Sancho carried the necessary weight and flesh for shipment, and in time he was gathered into the beef herd.

'I'm glad to see you, ol' boy,' were Bill's words of greeting, 'but I'm a little afraid this trip'll be a sad one for me, and a fatal one for you. You've managed to give us the slip lots of times just for fun. Well, now's the time you'd better limber up them legs and make a run for yo'r own hide.'

But Sancho displayed no indication that he would ever try to get away again. Upon the day they passed the Buzzard X range and the drive started for the shipping point, Bill missed Sancho from his customary place in the lead. A commotion among the cattle in the rear attracted his attention. The next instant, Sancho hove into sight, bucking and bawling, twisting his back while he dug at the ground in a maddened rage. Then he quit the herd, veered across a side hill, and bored his way into a willow thicket with a cowboy hot on his heels.

Before the man had untangled himself from the willows, Sancho had already passed through and was now topping another side hill. When the cowboy overtook him, he refused to give way. The man crowded his horse close and then Sancho slid to a stop in a single bound. He turned sullenly and swung around with his horn pointed at the horse. The horse jumped aside and avoided the thrust, but the horn hooked under the cowboy's stirrup. Sancho tossed his head up and the cowboy was lifted from the saddle and thrown to the ground. Before he could remount and give chase, Sancho had piled down a crumbling bank into a deep coulee. The cowboy's horse refused to take the jump, and before he could find a trail to follow the coulee, Sancho was securely hidden in another willow thicket. While the cowboy thrashed about in the brush, Sancho was standing quietly behind a screen of leaves, endeavoring to lick at welts of raised hair, moist with a strange-smelling liquid along the ridge of his backbone.

'Good ol' Sancho,' sighed Bill with relief, as he saw the cowboy returning empty-handed. 'When I was about to give up, you showed yo'r mettle and come through at the right time, and you done it fair and square too. When a steer runs rings around a cowhand like Artie Mayburn — he's entitled to his freedom. You had me sort of fooled for a while, but a feller never can tell what a wise ol' outlaw steer is apt to do.' Bill finished his musing with a chuckle.

Bill did not know that the sympathetic mind of Bud West had been working, and that he had ridden alongside the lazy steer and sprinkled his back with turpentine. When deprived of air, the liquid had set up a blistering heat worse than a branding iron, and had in turn set Sancho upon his fighting rampage!

When fall work was completed, the army of line riders scattered out in their various camps over the country, while the managers and owners surrendered themselves to an easy winter in town. Bill Sanders did not return to his lonely cabin among the weaving pines of the divide, but took up winter quarters at the Buzzard X. He had passed on to the position of general foreman.

Down in Beaverpond, Cliff Collins and a friend lounged in the Long Horn Saloon. The day was young and they were the only patrons in the building. Behind the bar, Charlie, the corpulent bartender, stood in his flowing white apron, polishing glasses. Charlie was thinking of his friends — yes, many of them — but at that time he was thinking of one in particular who had proven to be a friend in need. He recalled with vividness how one had responded. He had needed five hundred dollars badly, and Bill Sanders had advanced the sum without security or question. The debt had been paid, but Charlie had not forgotten. And now, he realized that the two men seated at the table were undoubtedly thinking of the same man.

'You've got a good man,' remarked the stranger to Collins. 'I've watched that fellow Sanders at work, and he surely knows his business.'

'Yes, that's right,' agreed Collins. 'It was a lucky day for me and the Buzzard X when I got hold of him. Not barring any — he's the best cowman that ever forked a horse — but he's got one weakness. He's sentimental.'

'I wouldn't think so,' replied the stranger. 'He looks to me like he'd go through hell and high water.'

'He would that,' explained Collins, 'but his weakness lies in another direction. He formed an attachment for an old outlaw steer that he drove up from Texas with the Tree Top herd, and that steer has not been shipped out to market yet. It's a sort of a standing joke around the ranch that he lets the steer get away on purpose.'

Charlie listened with interest at the discussion. When it appeared that Bill's integrity was being questioned, he felt moved to break the bartender's tradition of seeing all, hearing all, and agreeing with everything.

'Pouf!' he exclaimed indignantly. 'If that's so, why don't some other outfit gather that steer and ship 'im out? There's other fellers runnin' round-up wagons besides Bill Sanders. Didn't one of them J J punchers stand right there at the bar yesterday and tell me how his outfit followed Bill Sanders this fall, and run across a one-horned Tree Top steer with some blistered spots on his back? He says that steer come up fightin' like a wild cat, hooked two hosses, and come mighty nigh hookin' a man that he knocked off his hoss, just like I hear them tell about Art Mayburn.'

'No, no, Charlie. You misunderstood me,' Collins hastened to say. 'That steer and a hundred more like him wouldn't shake my faith in Bill Sanders. I just think it's kind of funny. If Bill feels better by keeping that old outlaw, he can do so just as long as I run the Buzzard X.'

'I'll just say this,' rejoined the other cowman. 'Any time you want to cut loose from Sanders — I'd like to have him take charge of my outfit up on the Rosebud.'

'You'll never get him as long as I've got anything to say,' rejoined Collins.

Charlie now beamed upon his customers. He brought forth his favorite brand of liquor, and set the bottle upon the bar with necessary glasses.

'I think it's time to cement them opinions with fittin' ceremony,' he said. 'Gents, walk up and pour out yo'r nose paint. This one is on me and the house.'

CHAPTER TWENTY-ONE

'IT AIN'T MY BUSINESS TO CAPTURE OUTLAWS'

D URING the following winter, Sancho returned to the line camp, but he received scant welcome from its occupants. He shifted his range, and the next fall he was grazing among the Antelope Hills, which headed one prong of the Big Dry.

Upon a crisp morning next October he lay in a peaceful doze absorbing warmth from the climbing sun rays banked against a sharp ridge at his back. A heavy coating of frost lay upon the wide expanse of prairie which rolled out in front of him. Spouts of steam formed upon his breath as it puffed from his nostrils in labored breathing.

A loud yell of human origin and the clatter of running cattle brought him out of his drowsy mood. Without raising his head, he flickered an eyelid half open and glimpsed a small bunch of cattle stringing along the hogback. He opened his eyes wider now and swept the open plain, where he saw other lines of cattle moving toward a central point.

Sancho hated to move from his comfortable position, much less go sprawling down steep hillsides as other cattle were doing and as he had playfully done many, many times before. He much preferred to remain in his warm bed. Knowledge from his lengthy experience, however, told him that he could not remain undisturbed — so he did the next best thing. He hid.

Sancho's age, topped off by two years in Montana, was now showing its effect upon him. Two winters of breathing the thin air of frosty temperatures and two summers of overfeeding had expanded his large frame into nearly fourteen hundred pounds of bone and sinew and fat. Thick layers of tallow bulged under his hide, stretched over a body that rounded off like a huge barrel. Heavy pods of fat clung to his sides and flanks where a sprinkling of gray hairs blended his color into a frosty red. A solid collar of white encircled his neck, tracing the scar left by the tree forks in which he had been imprisoned so long ago. A series of thick wrinkles surrounded the base of his one horn, which spiraled from his head to a length of three feet. All of his old Tree Top mates had gone out to market, and truly Sancho's carcass was long overdue on the butcher's block. He was now living on borrowed time.

Sancho had not been quick enough in hiding, for he soon found a mounted man riding into his grove of scrub pines, swinging an ever-ready rope. In spite of the urgent pressure that the cowboy brought upon him, he took his own time. The old-time spring of muscles was gone, and he felt overburdened by his ponderous weight. Therefore, he made his way carefully down the hill at a sidling angle on stiffened legs whose joints refused to limber up.

It was Bill Sanders who had floated a herd of a thousand beef steers around the foot of Antelope Hills and camped six miles below the divide rim. One more round-up and fifty miles of trail lay between him and the shipping point. One more herd to ship, and the end of the year's work. Therefore an air of hilarity clung to his men as he flung out his riders over the head draws and canyons of the Big Dry the morning that Sancho was gathered into the round-up.

During the trip to the shipping point Bill waited in hope for Sancho to make another spectacular break for liberty, but the break never came. Lazy indifference and sluggishness bore plain evidence that all of his cunning and daring spirit had been smothered by age and obesity. Bill felt as if an unkind trick had been played upon him when fate decreed that he must be the one to direct the movement that was sending Sancho to his doom. Besides the regret of driving Sancho to his death, other matters worried him. He was on the verge of a break with the Buzzard X management.

During the interval between the break of winter and coming of spring, while cattle were beginning to slip dead hair and cowboys were looking forward to the general round-up — the traders had also been active. A group of Eastern capitalists had come into ownership of the Buzzard X and all that went with it. Bill's friend Cliff Collins had been replaced as general manager by a young banker who boasted his intentions to wring increased profits from the outfit. His knowledge of cattle and range affairs was a joke to Bill and his men, but they admitted he was versed in the science of efficiency and that he had a knack of figuring expenses down to the limit. It was his mustache, however, not his cold-blooded business policies, that impressed the cowboys and branded him a dude. On more than one occasion he and Bill clashed over the policy of operating the outfit. Now, their differences over Sancho opened up an unbridgeable chasm between them.

'It ain't altogether sentiment with me, that I want to save him,' Bill had argued. 'That steer is worth his keep any time. He can lead a herd across a swim-min' river or through a badland gulch and save lots of time and hossflesh.'

'Perhaps so,' was the cool response, 'but I pay cowboys to drive cattle, and if they can't do it without keeping a leader steer I'll get some men who can. That animal you are soft about represents only so much beef on the hoof, and getting him to the scales is my only concern. It surprises me that a man holding your position would give way to maudlin' sentiment. You must be losing your grip of things.'

Thus, in the first bitter and resentful mood of his entire life, Bill camped his outfit on the north bank of the Yellowstone and prepared to swim the herd over next day.

While they were catching up their night horses, a man wearing the badge of authority approached them. 'I'm the sheriff,' he said tersely. 'We've got a couple of train robbers cornered in the badlands some'ers hereabout, and I want as many men and hosses as I can git together. I aim to make a drive through the hills tomorrow.'

'I cain't spare any men,' Bill said shortly. 'I've got to put this herd across that river and I'll need ever' man I can swing in line. That water is cold and it's runnin' full of slush ice, and them beeves won't take it very easy.'

The sheriff looked with a vacant stare across the sloughing river to the railroad track and busy stockyards, where a train of loaded cars was pulling away and another engine stood with a string of empties ready to load.

'Put off crossin' for a couple of days and help me round up that gang. We cut their trail over on the Missouri and killed one and their pack hoss. I could git 'em hemmed tomorrow if I had help.'

Bill let his gaze follow the sheriff's, and he looked at a line of empty cars on the siding a half-mile west of the stockyards. Then he turned to the sheriff, shaking his head.

'I'm sorry, sheriff,' he said. 'I cain't put off crossin'. My cars are all ready and there's a rush. I've got to take my turn at loadin'.'

'Yeah, that's the trouble with you cowmen,' the sheriff spat. 'When it's a train robbed of twenty thousand dollars — you don't give a damn. But I bet if anybody yanked a single pony out of yo'r string — you'd be snappin' at his heels like a pack of blood hounds——'

'Twenty thous——,' echoed Bud West. 'Boy! If I ever git my hands on that much kale, I'd——'

'Grantin' you're right, sheriff,' Bill said with a slight gesture of impatience, 'we still got plenty troubles that just come natural without stirrin' up more. As long as them fellers rob trains and banks it ain't none of our business. They could ruin us in a single night if they wanted to. They could drop a match in our grass and burn it all off, or round up a bunch of our hosses and go south with 'em. It ain't my business to capture outlaws.'

'All right,' acquiesced the officer. 'I've heard so much of that kind of talk lately that I'm about ready to believe it myself.'

The sheriff turned in his saddle and looked over the two hundred head of saddle horses in the rope corral. 'There's one thing I want to tell you about,' he said, tapping the tail of his quirt against his boot-top. 'We've crowded them robbers so close that their hosses is all in. They cain't go very far without fresh ones. Be shore and put enough men with yo'r ponies tonight to hold 'em.'

'Bud,' spoke Bill sharply, 'you heard what he said. Pick up three men to help the night wrangler. Tell 'em there's a couple of fellers loose in the country that could use some rested hossflesh. Tell 'em, if anybody comes snoopin' around tonight, not to stand on ceremony — just shoot, and ask questions later. They're paid for. We ain't out to exterminate train robbers, but when they git to monkeyin' with Buzzard X stock — it's a hoss of a different color.'

Bill sat apart from his men in camp that night — busy with his own thoughts. One thing was certain now. He would cut loose from the Buzzard X as soon as the herd was shipped. He had never been out of a job in his life, and he wondered how he would go about getting another. He would never have suspected that a dozen outfits in eastern Montana would like to have him.

As he pondered about his future, his thoughts reverted to the past. A dismal sadness crept into his heart. He thought of Sancho — but not alone of Sancho.

'She asked me to take care of him,' he muttered. 'But it ain't no use to grieve over spilt milk. She's done forgot all about me and ol' Sancho too. I guess she's married that bank clerk or somebody else. There's too many other fellers different from me — rich and educated — to let her run around loose very long. I wasn't never meant for her nohow. I'm close on to thirty-two years old. I've been poundin' a hoss's back ever since I was a kid, and ain't got nothin' to show for it but a lot of ignorance. She'd never have no use for a long-haired fogy like me that don't know nothin' except to cap off a bronco hoss or rap a bunch of dogies over the trail.'

Bill's spell was broken into by the gay bantering of his men as they turned the cards and discussed their own future plans. Three of them were going to Chicago with the shipment of cattle. They were mirthfully outlining a proposed conquest of the city upon their arrival. Others were planning happy reunions with families and friends in different sections of the country. Bill smiled grimly at the mental picture he painted. Those bound for Chicago, he acknowledged, would doubtless see their plans fulfilled. The immediate departure of the train after loading would not permit diversion. But the others? Bill could see them in a riotous celebration which would last as long as their money. Then he could see them come straggling back to the ranch — broke and unrepentant — to spend the winter and start out next spring to plan all over again.

'The trouble with me and Sancho,' mumbled Bill, 'the trouble with both of us — we're gittin' old and 've lost our snap.'

He sat in bitter meditation, and familiar sounds floated in to him out of the night. He heard the call of a lobo wolf far away in the badlands, announcing that he had struck down some luckless animal and he was inviting all of his kind to share the feast with him. Across the canyon he heard the singing voice of his men as they circled around the herd. Behind him in a wide sag, he heard the sharp crack of the night wrangler's whip upon a straying horse. To his left the dark waters of the Yellowstone gurgled softly as they slid by in the deep shadows.

He listened and correctly placed each sound. The mask of uncertainty was crowded from his face by a look of determined intention. He closed his jaws with a snap and once more became the resourceful Bill Sanders.

He arose, and with a backward glance at the group of joking men strode from the circle of campfire light. He mounted his coal-black night horse, called Pitter-Patter because of a habit of slapping his feet down sharply when excited or spurred to sudden action. The noise of Pitter-Patter's hoofs faded away as Bill rode into the yawning darkness.

Next morning the cattle were loaded and started upon their fatal journey. That night, the Buzzard X men were celebrating with proper ceremony, enjoying pleasures of bright lights for the first time in months. Toying over their fifth drink, Bud West and Art May-burn found that they had many questions to discuss and settle.

'An' what about ol' Sancho gittin' away last night?' Art asked half accusingly. 'I've heard it sort of whispered around,' he added, 'that Feather Lip says he's goin' to fire the men that was on guard when Sancho departed away and therefrom.'

'Yeah, I've heard that same gossip floatin' around,' Bud admitted. 'But I don't give a tinker's damn what Feather Lip says or does,' he hurried to continue. 'I aim to quit the outfit anyhow, and if he fires me — he'll git that lickin' just a little quicker.'

Bud looked challengingly around the saloon and then returned to his companion across the table. 'I'll tell you what I'm goin' to do, cowboy,' he said. 'I'm goin' to start in at the ground and work up. I'm goin' to slap that dude's head to a peak and then knock it off. When I git through, that soft face of his'n'll look like it'd been run through a sausage mill.'

Bud stood up and looked over the room again. 'I wish he was here now,' he said. 'I'd show you what a cowhand can do to a dude. I'm goin' to quit,' he roared, slapping his hand against the table. 'There's too many good outfits in this country for a feller to waste his time workin' for a cheap one like this has got to be.'

'But you've departed from the subject,' reminded Art gently. 'You ain't told me nothin' about ol' Sancho yet.'

'Well, there ain't much to tell,' replied Bud. 'I cain't figger out how Feather Lip is goin' to find out anything. He was at the hotel asleep and I was right on the ground — and I'll be damned if I can tell a speck about it myself.'

Bud hitched up his chair closer and leaned over the table, as though he had a confidential communication to make. 'You see it's like this,' he half whispered. 'I first heard a whoosh and a whish and a whack. Then I hear somethin' grunt and go snff. Then a movin' mountain with a white face come heavin' at me. I don't want to git crushed by a mountain slide, so I give a little room, and let it go by. Then somethin' darts past me so fast it looks like a string of black hosses.'

'Was that all?' questioned Art.

'Not quite,' resumed Bud. 'Somethin' tore off up that canyon thumpin' the ground like a drum major. I ain't lost nothin' up that canyon that I care anything about — so I just stayed where I was and tended to business.'

'Could them sounds you spoke of been made by ol' Pitter-Patter?' asked Art.

'Seems like he's made similar commotions when Bill got excited and ripped the spurs into 'im,' replied Bud. 'But what we losin' time about this for?' he asked impatiently. 'We got too much else to do. Hey, Charlie!' he called. 'Fill 'em up agin.'

CHAPTER TWENTY-TWO

'I'VE GOT A DEBT
TO SETTLE'

WITH the satisfaction that comes to a man with his work well done, Bill Sanders reveled in freedom from responsibility for the first time in years. He stood on the uneven board sidewalk and watched the street activities in the bustling little cow town. The knock of heavy loaded wagons thudded along the single driveway, while bearded drivers lashed sullen ox teams with tongue and whip. The sharp clatter of light vehicles chopped the frosty air; horse teams shied at strange surroundings and pranced nervously at the shrill whistles and hoarse shouts. Mingling with the clank of draft gear and creak of harness leather was the foot patter of many saddle horses, the jingle of spurs, and the clamp of bridle bits as mounted and pedestrian cowboys swarmed in the crowded area where teamsters jockeyed for position at loading platforms.

Out of the confusion of human beings and moving horses, Bill saw the sheriff approaching.

'Our drive didn't git us nowhere yesterday,' the sheriff said. 'We was too short-handed. Them robbers is out in them hills some'ers yet and I want you to lead a posse today,' he continued. 'I've got a line of men behind 'em and a patrol ridin' the river bank to shoo 'em back if they try to swim out. You know that country like a book over there,' he said with a sweep of his hand, indicating the Yellowstone badlands, 'and we'll git 'em today if you'll come along and lead circle.'

Bill hesitated before replying — and then he said: 'All right, sheriff. It ain't exactly my business to hunt outlaws, but I'll do it this time if——,'

Bill was interrupted by a man on horseback forging his way excitedly along the street and stopping in front of where he and the sheriff were talking.

'One of the river guards,' the sheriff explained, turning to the man.

'They's somethin' lodged on a gravel bar in the river,' the man said in a shrill voice. 'It's a hoss and saddle, and a man's body is layin' across the saddle. I was afeared to risk swimmin' out to it in that cold water, so I——'

'We'll see what that is first,' the sheriff said with quick decision. 'Maybe this boy has found what we're lookin' for.'

The sheriff secured a canoe and had it hauled to the place indicated by the river guard. Two of his recruited possemen rowed out to the object and fastened long ropes to it and returned to shore.

'It ain't no hoss,' one of them remarked as he started hauling away on the rope. 'It's a cow. And it ain't no man laying across the saddle neither. It's a pack of two slickers — a blanket and a little grub.'

They pulled on the rope and floated the carcass of the dead animal closer to shore. Bill recognized the head as it bobbed in and out of the water displaying a single horn. Slowly he backed away while the crowd hurried up to view the body of Sancho with a saddle buckled upon his back.

'We've got 'em now,' the sheriff remarked with a satisfied grin. 'When fellers take to saddlin' up cow stock they're gittin' desp'rate for transportation. They're hidin' out around here some'ers without any grub and one or both of 'em is afoot. That is' — he paused in his speech and gazed with fascination at the rolling water of the river—'that is,' he finished, pointing to the water, 'unless they're out there.'

Bill took one look at the pack ropes and cinches imbedded in Sancho's flanks and he shuddered. He could picture the misery of the courageous old steer as he heaved and panted for breath against the binding pressure when he tried to inflate his lungs for swimming. Bill could see him still fighting even after he was under water, until the last spark of life was gone.

Bill closed his eyes and made a silent vow to hunt down the men responsible and take their lives in payment for Sancho's.

'He's a whopper,' the sheriff commented. 'I cain't see why he didn't make the river. That load ain't too heavy for an ox his size.'

'He never had a chance,' Bill replied decisively. 'Them pack ropes and saddle cinches was drawed so tight they cut off his wind. When a steer swims he's got to have room to swell out and keep afloat.'

'Go slow, there!' the sheriff spoke sharply to one of the possemen who started to untie the pack ropes. 'We don't know who them fellers is yet, and we might find a lead in some of this outfit. We want to save ever'thing and look it over close.'

Bill stood aside and remained silent while the sheriff leaned over the dead steer and inspected the pack and trappings. He looked carefully at the peculiarity of the knotted ropes before untying them. He examined the slickers and blanket, and then turned his attention to the saddle and bridle.

'We're learnin' a little,' he mused. 'The man that tied that pack on come from a brushy country. He used what's called the stirrup hitch. It holds both ends of the pack under a hoss's belly and keeps brush from tearin' it to pieces. The saddle bears out that the'ry too. The maker's stamp has been scraped off, but it's a double rig that's made in the south where they do heavy ropin'. There ain't no saddles made in this country like that. He must be a little man, too. Them stirrups is purty short.'

While the sheriff was voicing his own deductions, Bill's eyes were taking in other things that the sheriff had overlooked. 'Them hoss-hair cinches are handmade and the weave is genuine Spanish,' was Bill's mental comment.

'Ain't that a fine piece o' work!' the sheriff continued. He had unhooked from the saddle-horn a riding quirt and was holding it up for the crowd to see the skillful handiwork that had brought the mysterious loops and sensuous whorls together into the twelve-strand braid of grained rawhide strings.

But Bill's thoughts had now reverted to the past. He could recall the fierce scowl of a lanky Mexican who leaned with one side propped against a bed roll in the edge of a campfire light. He remembered how nimble and certain the man's fingers had worked, darting in and out of the maze of tangled strings, braiding them together into a riding quirt. Bill knew the owner of the outfit as well as though Ben Harte's name had been drawn upon it with capital letters.

'The cold-blooded hound!' Bill muttered. 'I'll hunt him down and kill him like I would a wolf. He killed old Sancho without givin' him a chance.'

A close search of the river bank failed to reveal tracks where either man or horse had waded from the stream. The posse started back for town, to cross over on the ferry and search the north bank.

'We'd better eat first,' the sheriff remarked as they entered the town and he squinted at the position of the sun. 'There ain't no tellin' where this hunt will lead us to.'

Bill stopped a block from the hotel on the pretense of loosening his cinch and resetting his saddle. Before the possemen were all seated at the crowded dining-table, he was being ferried over the river alone.

'I'll not stop to eat,' he thought to himself. 'I've got a debt to settle with Mr. Harte first.'

He rode quickly to the point opposite where Sancho had been lodged in the river, and took up a trail. An hour later, while the sheriff and posse stood gathered around and puzzled over the lifeless body of a Mexican, Bill was miles up the canyon and the sun was getting low.

Bill had followed a slight drag a few paces from the river bank and found Juan's body with a bullet hole in the back of his head. The fact that the Mexican had been shot from behind and an attempt made to conceal his body was ample proof that he had been murdered in cold blood.

Further examination of the ground showed Bill a freshly made horse track leading up a deep canyon. A mile further on, he came upon a single horse standing dejectedly in the creek bed — a forlorn testimonial of cruelty at its worst. Cakes of dirty salt from dried sweat covered his body. His gaunt flanks and bony sides indicated he had suffered long rides without adequate food. Raw scalds along his back told of long hours under saddle. Dried blood from shoulder to flank told of vicious cuts of spur rowels showing forcing of speed and endurance that was unnatural. He held his right foreleg in front at a delicate tension. There was still a flash in his bulging eyes and a tint of snuff-brown coloring to his body, but Bill had to decipher out the deuce of hearts brand before he was certain of his identification. Closer inspection showed the horse's right shoulder to be broken.

Bill's eyes strayed to the ground, where he saw evidence of a violent struggle. Horse tracks mingled with hoof prints of a large bovine animal. Marks on the ground indicated that a horse had fallen at one time during the contest, and at another spot were signs of where the bovine animal had lain. Bill chewed at the tip end of his bridle rein as he hastened to reconstruct the desperate state of affairs that had forced men to the expedient of saddling and packing a wild steer to ford a river, and then one to murder the other in failure of the attempt to make their plans succeed.

'I've got it now,' he mused. 'Their hosses was give' out. They was afraid to try to swim the river and carry their grub and bedding. They run across ol' Sancho, and Harte remembered how he could swim. Harte roped Sancho and he jerked the *grullo* down and broke his shoulder. Then they had to do somethin'. They started to swim the river, and they buckled the cinches and pulled the pack ropes so tight that Sancho drowned. Harte got out some way — and then he decided that one might git away on one hoss but two couldn't. So he just killed the Mexican and thought he'd double back on his trail like a coyote. The lowdown snake! I'll choke him to death like he did Sancho,' Bill growled.

Bill then turned to the horse. Although the afternoon was a typical Indian summer day, the animal was shivering with convulsive rigors. His broken shoulder was badly swollen, and at Bill's approach the *grullo* hopped one step and whinnied with pain. Bill could hear the crunch of bones when the right leg dragged across the ground.

Bill's face paled and his eyes narrowed. He murmured an indistinct oath with a glance up the trail. He pulled his gun from its holster and leveled it at the suffering horse.

'I hate to do this, old feller,' he said, 'but it's the only way out for you. One quick flash and yo'r sufferin' will be over.'

Bill replaced the empty shell in his gun with a loaded one. He stood over the dead horse and looked pityingly down at him. 'I just hope that I can put the next one into the man that used to own you,' he said, turning away and mounting his own horse.

Bill followed along the trail, and at intervals found signs that were encouraging. The imprint of a boot track now and then up a steep incline told him that the horse he was following was very tired, and that the rider was endeavoring to conserve its strength. He was convinced that ere long the horse would have to rest.

At the approach of darkness, Bill left the canyon gulch and rode to the foot of a pointed butte to spend the night. He now found himself in the same unhappy state that he thought the man to be in that he was following. He had no food; his thin coat was sadly inadequate to keep out the night chill; and fearing discovery, he dared not build a fire.

Through the long night while he shivered beside his grazing horse, he noted now and then that the animal ceased grazing and pointed his ears knowingly toward a certain spot in the canyon below. He knew that the horse was hearing some sound that was not audible to human ears. At dawn, he saw a thin wisp of smoke break out of the canyon brush and spiral heavenward.

'I think our trails are about to cross for the last time, Mr. Ben Harte,' he muttered grimly.

Bill swung his saddle upon the horse and pulled the cinch tight. He tested the steadiness of the saddle, and pulled his gun from its scabbard and rolled the cylinder. He replaced the gun, stepped into his stirrup, and rode down into the canyon to meet Ben Harte.

Lest the sound of his horse's feet betray his presence, Bill held the animal to a slow walk. When he came in sight, Harte was squatting on his heels, rubbing his hands together over the remains of a small fire. The front of his hat brim dipped low and almost touched the point of his hawk nose. His beady eyes were hidden from view. His once-trimmed beard had grown wild, and now covered his lower face in a matted sheaf. A strip of fresh rabbit skin hung on a bush behind him, and the charred remains of meat clinging to picked bones of the carcass indicated that he had lately indulged in an unsavory breakfast. His horse with drooping head stood saddled at his side.

Bill swung to the ground and leveled his pistol as Harte looked up.

'Stand up and fight, Ben! Grab that gun — I'm goin' to give you one chance——'

'Don't! Don't!' begged Harte, while he sank to his knees and held out his hands as if to fend off the expected bullet.

Bill took a step toward the cowering desperado; the point of his gun lowered and hung at his hip. 'Git up!' he commanded. 'I'll give you a chance — but I'm goin' to shoot you full of holes.'

Harte suddenly jumped to his feet and swung his small body into the saddle. With a deft twist of bridle reins, he whirled the animal around and was galloping away up the trail before he had settled into position. He leaned over the saddle-horn and plied whip and spur to the jaded animal. Bill raised his gun and drew a bead on the back of his head. His thumb drew back on the hammer and his finger touched the trigger. Then his tension relaxed and the muzzle of the weapon lowered, and he let the hammer settle again into its seat.

'I cain't shoot a man in the back,' he murmured. 'But there's somethin' better that I can do. He murdered Juan. They hang a man for cold-blooded murder. I will let the law give him the same dose he give pore old Sancho.'

He remounted and gave chase, shaking the coils of his rope into a loop as he ran along. His horse gained easily upon Harte's tired one, and he was soon within throwing distance. Once Harte turned as though he intended to draw his gun and fight it out, but he leaned forward again and resumed his merciless whipping and spurring.

With two quick whirls around his head, Bill's loop sailed out and dropped over the shoulders of the fleeing outlaw. His horse came to a sudden stop and Harte was jerked from the saddle. Before he could recover his breath, Bill had pounced upon him. It took but a moment to snatch the gun and tie Harte's hands. As he was preparing to place Harte again upon the horse, freshly cut stitches in the outlaw's saddle skirt attracted his attention. His probing fingers between the sheepskin lining and skirt leather extracted bill after bill of currency. The off side yielded a like amount.

Bill stacked the currency together and bound it with a small string which he unraveled from his saddle blanket.

'A good-sized day's work,' commented Bill, surveying the money. 'I haven't counted it, but I suppose you got Juan's share too.'

'Yeah,' said Harte, 'I have. He won't need any where——'
Then he checked his speech.

'Go ahead,' prompted Bill. 'Go ahead and say he won't need any where he's gone to. You'd just as well own up to it now.'

CHAPTER TWENTY-THREE

A MONUMENT
FOR SANCHO

B ILL turned his prisoner and loot over to the sheriff, and after a sound sleep he emerged from a late breakfast next morning feeling both lost and satisfied. He felt that he had done a good day's work when he settled for Sancho and placed Harte behind jail bars — and he felt lost because for the first time in his life he was without employment. He stood there upon the sidewalk little dreaming that events were swiftly approaching that would change his future life.

First came Buddie West, tearing along up the street riding a strange horse. He slid the animal to a stop directly in front of Bill, and standing in his stirrups he raised his elbows and twisted his body sidewise like a model on display. The gay cowboy was rigged out in the most fashionable attire of clothing that the times afforded. An expensive hat of white beaver fur with wide brim and pointed crown sat tilted upon the back of his head. A fine-threaded coat with fur trimmings flared open and disclosed the fancy beadwork front of a yellow vest of soft buckskin. A pair of light checked trousers of the best California weave flowed downward and tucked into the legs of scrolled Morocco-topped boots. A pair of brand new silver-mounted spurs jingled from his heels, and the legs of bat-wing chaps with their bright conches and fancy string lacing straddled the front of his saddle fork.

'Kind of bushin' out, ain't you, Bud?' Bill smiled as he ran his eye appraisingly over the new outfit.

'Ain't, though?' came the hearty response. 'Pardner, I been waitin' a long time for my day and I got it last night. I showed them gamblers in this town a trick they never seen before.'

Bud settled in his saddle, and raked his hand caressingly over the horse's mane before resuming his conversation.

'They're gittin' so many of us Texas fellers up here that likes to play monte,' he confided, 'that they opened up a game in the Palace Saloon. They imported a kind of a dude slicker from down about Fort Worth to deal. I cleaned that game's bank roll last night like a brake shoe cleans mud from a wagon wheel. Before that slick-fingered gambler knowed what was goin' on, I'd touched 'im for two hundred and fifty good old American cartwheels——'

'But what you doin' on that horse?' asked Bill, looking at the Speer brand on the animal's shoulder. 'Did you win him in the game too?'

'No,' replied Bud, 'but that's what I stopped to tell you about. I quit the Buzzard X, and I wound up my services by givin' that feather-lipped dude the thrashin' of his whole life. He's nursin' some black eyes and loose teeth today. I'm on my way to the Speer outfit up on the Sandstone. I'm goin' to work for them awhile. What you goin' to do now, Bill?' he asked.

Bill looked out into the busy street before he answered.

'I don't know, Bud. I just don't know,' he said slowly. 'I might lay around town all winter and pick up what I can grab onto in the spring.'

'You needn't worry, old pardner,' Bud said with assurance. 'I wish I had yo'r chances in this country. Any of these outfits around here would be glad to take you on.'

A crowd of men riding horses with a speer on their left shoulder came galloping noisily up the street. Bud pulled up his bridle reins and leaned sidewise to catch Bill's hand.

'Good-bye, old pardner,' he said. 'I'll leave you now, but I'll never forget you.'

He straightened in his stirrups, removed his hat and with a wide sweep and a loud 'Whoo-oo-ee!' touched spurs to his horse's side. The animal sprang forward into a gallop; Bud threw his weight to his right stirrup, and as he raced away he turned around and looked back at Bill. 'I'll meet you here when work is done next fall. And don't take any wooden nickels,' he called back gaily over his shoulder.

Bill watched Bud join the Speer men and disappear from sight around a bend of the road. He turned away, and the sheriff approached him again.

'I guess I'd orter congratulate you,' the officer said, extending his hand. 'I'll own that I was a bit peeved when I first learnt you'd give us the slip and gone off on a sheriffin' expedition of yo'r own — but now I can see the sense of yo'r move. A thousand-dollar reward ain't to be sniffed at any time,' he continued, pulling a roll of bills from his pocket.

Bill held out both hands in a deprecating gesture. 'But sheriff,' he protested, 'you got me wrong. I ain't no head-hunter. My motives was all personal. He drowned my old pet steer. I aimed to hunt that feller down and kill 'im like I would a snake, but he run and I couldn't shoot nobody in the back——'

'Yes, I know,' interrupted the sheriff. 'I *sabe* all that — but you ain't got no scruples agin takin' a thousand dollars for yo'r trouble, have you? The railroad offered the reward for the capture, and I'm more'n glad to pay it out of their money that you brought in. I'm tickled to death to git that gang broke up. Take this thousand. It might come in handy some day,' he said forcibly as he again extended the roll of bills.

'Not much!' said Bill emphatically. 'That'd be blood money, sheriff, and I ain't after any of it.'

In the lapse of silence that followed, Bill started with a sudden thought. 'I'll tell you what to do with that money,' he said.

'You take it and have a monument built for old Sancho out there,' and he pointed to a peak rising alone from the level plains.

'It's a go,' said the sheriff with hearty approval. 'I'd feel better myself. The steer's entitled to it, anyhow.'

'It's a go,' repeated the sheriff solemnly as he shook Bill's hand. 'I'll have a statue of that old steer cut from solid rock.'

CHAPTER TWENTY-FOUR

BILL GETS A LETTER

WHEN Bill turned to leave the sheriff, he was startled at the sound of a voice behind him. A voice with an elusive familiarity about it.

'Mr. Sanders,' it said.

Bill tried to remember when it was that he had been addressed as mister before. Full of curiosity he turned to look into the face of Freddie Williams.

Old memories, old animosities stirred within him. Then Bill's sporting instinct and fairness arose above his prejudice.

'I didn't come up to standard — and she took her pick' flashed through his mind while he returned to normal civility.

The smile had faded from Freddie's face.

'Don't you know me?' he asked uncertainly. 'I'm Fred Williams. I used to know you down in Texas.' Then as Bill suddenly extended his hand in greeting a sheepish grin appeared upon Freddie's face. 'The last time we parted was over a water trough,' he smiled.

Bill grinned also. 'I didn't ever expect to see you here, Freddie. What are you doing in this country, anyhow?'

But Bill was giving little heed to his own words. Other burning questions were coursing through his mind. A hurried appraisal of the man before him indicated that Freddie was in prosperity. His stylishly tailored clothes were expensive and loud. The sparkle of his eye and clear skin showed no hint of dissipation. But still there were deep lines around his mouth and eyes that were not natural. At least they told a story of long hours at keen concentration, and the twitching of his fingers indicated nervousness. Now disconcerting and uneasy thoughts arose. Could these signs of premature aging be lines of sorrow caused by the death of some one dear to him? The only person in the world that Bill thought could be dear to any one was Virginia Lowe. He steeled himself to ask a question that he dreaded to have answered.

'How's Vir — er, I mean Miss Lowe?' he stammered.

The expression on Freddie's face spoke his surprise at the question.

'You ought to know if anybody does,' he commented drily.

While Bill remained in a blank silence, Freddie jerked one side of his coat around to his body with a nervous movement and continued:

'I got my walking papers next day after the water-trough affair, and I haven't seen her since.'

Freddie now turned his eyes from Bill and looked away into space.

'You see, our meeting turned out to be a sad event for us both. She cried a little and then walked up and put her hand upon my shoulder and said: "Freddie. There's a misunderstanding all around. You could be a nice boy if you tried — but the man I love could go into that gambling place and come out without being sent for." Then,' continued Freddie, 'she walked out of the room with her head up like a queen and her eyes shining like the stars — with me standing there like a fool.'

Freddie dug into his pocket and produced a pack of cigarettes. His nervous fingers tore off the end wrapper and he extended the opened package to Bill, who shook his head. While Freddie was lighting his cigarette, Bill drew a long sigh.

'You see,' Freddie continued, 'she knew more than I thought she did. I learned that her interest in me was only to straighten me out because of friendship she had for my family.'

'After that,' he said, 'I decided to humor the gambling streak in me and get on the winning side, so I turned professional. I'm dealing a monte game at the Palace Saloon now.'

Then, as if he realized that he had broken the code of the tight-lipped gambler, Freddie stopped in his speech. He started to leave, then he half turned around again.

'Drop in on me some time,' he said. 'If there's anything in the joint you want, just help yourself. I'll never be able to repay the favor you did me when you dropped me in the water trough.'

His voice carried a ring of sincerity as he walked away.

For a while Bill leaned against an awning post and tried to assemble his fluttering thoughts. He became aware that some one was calling his name, and out of the maze he saw the bartender, Charlie, standing in front of his saloon three doors away. He was beckoning to Bill with an oblong square of paper in his hand.

'Here's a letter the Buzzard X cook left yesterday,' he said as Bill entered the saloon, and Charlie handed it to him and then took up his station behind the bar.

It took no expert deduction for Bill to recognize the handwriting upon the envelope. He had seen his name written on checks with that quaint style of penmanship many times. He opened the letter hurriedly, and while reading it he was unconscious of a convulsive twitching of his mouth corners. When he finished, he crushed the paper. His hands grasped the bar. A mist came into his eyes.

'What's the matter, Bill?' asked Charlie in alarm, developing a sudden spryness and vaulting over the bar. 'Is it bad news? Can I help out any? You know, Bill — I'm with you right or wrong,' he said hurriedly.

'No, Charlie. It ain't bad news,' said Bill in a throaty voice. 'It just sort of upset me — that's all.'

His eyes came to rest upon the neat row of bottles and glasses upon the back bar. 'Let's have a drink,' he ordered peremptorily.

The perplexed Charlie receded into his shell of reserve and walked thoughtfully around the end of the bar to his place behind it. He eyed Bill curiously, watching him pour out and down a glass filled with whiskey to the brim.

'It's funny about things,' Bill mumbled. 'I thought I was all forgot about — let's have another.' A grim smile wound its way onto his face. He raised his eyes to Charlie and their glasses met above the bar. 'We ain't likely to have many more together,' he finished.

'Now we'll have one on the house,' returned Charlie in friendliness. 'Then I think I'd better call a doc and have 'im examine yo'r head. They's somethin' bad out of tune.'

'Charlie,' said Bill, 'did you ever hear of the Southern Cross?'

'Shore. I've heard of the Southern Cross lots of times. I ain't been a low-down barkeep all my life. I used to be a respectable cowhand just like you. I used to stand guard with a feller that had studied astronomy and he said——'

'All right,' interrupted Bill. 'If anybody asks you where I am, you can tell 'em that I'm tryin' to put my horse's head under the Southern Cross.'

Bill strode from the saloon, and Charlie watched him walk across a vacant lot to a livery stable. Within a half-hour he came out, riding one horse and leading another. A pack was tied on the lead horse. He rode down the main street and turned off on a road that angled southeast. Charlie watched him disappear behind a shoulder of a hill.

Acting upon another sudden impulse, Charlie hurried around in front and picked up the crumpled letter where Bill had dropped it between the brass rail and bar. He smoothed out the wrinkled paper and glanced guiltily about him. He then refolded it and weighted it down upon the back bar with a glass. While he stood dividing his glances between the folded paper and the door, Cliff Collins sauntered into the saloon. Charlie served the ordered drink, but made frequent peeps at the letter behind him.

'You know anything about Bill Sanders before he come here?' he asked abruptly.

'N-o-o, not much,' was the disinterested reply. 'He came to me well recommended, though. Why?'

'W-e-ll,' said Charlie, scratching his thick mop of hair, 'they's been some funny things happened around here this mornin', and Bill's actin' kind of like he had a case of blind staggers. I thought he might be crowded a little. They's been more'n one of them Texas fellers hit this country that had to leave home in the nighttime.'

'Well, what makes you think Bill might be on the loose?' asked Collins, with the first interest he had shown in Charlie's problem.

Charlie folded his hands under his long apron and set his feet apart while his eyes focussed steadily upon Collins's face.

'First,' he said, 'a letter comes here to 'im yestiddy. I never heerd of Bill gittin' a letter before — but that ain't nothin' to git excited about. Most any kind of bowlegged cowpuncher is liable to git a letter some time. But next, I see 'im in a powwow with that flashy-dressed gambler at the Palace. That gambler comes from Texas just like Bill does. After that, I gives Bill his letter. He's about half wobbly when he comes in — but when he reads that letter he just goes up in blue smoke.'

Charlie paused in his recital and eyed Collins inquiringly. 'But this is the blowup,' continued Charlie. 'You know Bill never was a drinkin' man — but he poured hisself three stiff ones that'd stand me on my head — and he throwed 'em down without battin' a eye.'

Collins scratched his chin slowly and remained silent. 'He said it warn't bad news,' Charlie continued, 'but he shore didn't act like it was good. He dropped the letter on the floor when he went out, and it's on the back bar now.'

'It certainly takes you a long time to get around to anything, Charlie,' Collins said with impatience. 'What does the letter say?' Charlie averted his head and his breath came hard while he looked at Collins scornfully and he thundered:

'How'n the hell am I to know! I ain't runnin' around readin' other fellers' mail.'

'Excuse me,' said Collins turning his head to hide a smile. 'I just thought perhaps — where is Bill now?'

Charlie made a deprecating gesture and a wide sweep of his hand. 'He's out in the wide, wide country som'ers. He said we wasn't likely to have any more drinks together and then stampeded out of town. From the way he talked and acted he's liable to be headin' for South Africa or some other seaport.'

Charlie turned to the bar and splashed its shining surface with a towel. 'D'y s'pose Bill got tangled in some kind of trouble back in Texas, and that gambler and the letter give 'im a tip that there was some law hound on his trail?'

'H-m-m,' ruminated Collins. 'It is odd that Bill acted that way. I just can't say. Bill's a mighty good man, but I've seen some mighty good cowhands that couldn't afford to have their past exposed. I'll tell you what,' Collins said tactfully. 'I think the circumstances justify us in doing a little snooping. Let's get that letter and read it. If Bill is in trouble we both want to help him. I'll have to take his trail and bring him back. He's too good a man to be running away from anything. You get the letter and read it. I'll keep a lookout so nobody will catch us.'

Charlie secured the letter and read laboriously through its four pages of longhand.

'Phft!' he snorted, throwing it down on the bar. 'I'll say he's in trouble. He's in so deep he'll never swim out. He's plumb out of our reach. We couldn't drag 'im back with a log chain. Think what he's got hisself into. I knowed all the time he wasn't exactly right in the head.'

Charlie stood glaring at Collins in disgust. 'Here! Read it for yo'rself,' he commanded, pushing the letter toward Collins.

'I ain't got the heart to tell you what's in it. And when you git through, I'll have a stiff drink poured out to steady yo'r nerves.'

Collins picked up the letter and read aloud:

Wm. Sanders esq.
My esteemed friend Bill:

When the farmers started settling this country, all of us old fogies thought it was ruined, but we were wrong. It was just in the making. The old Tree Top outfit had a hard time to support me and about thirty of you cowboys. Now it is going to support several hundred families who will build towns and schools and churches.

I am having the ranch cut up into small tracts to sell to farmers and small cattlemen. Before an acre of ground is sold, I want all of the old Tree Top men to have a chance to buy a home and settle down. I am in a position to sell you the land on long-time payments and let you have the money to improve it and stock it with a small bunch of cattle. I am going to reserve the headquarter ranch and build me a home there.

The boys are having their hair trimmed once in a while now and are shining up to some of the fine girls that the settlers brought into the country. Dave Houston has about formed a truce with the old farmer down on the river, and from indications he and Katie will be the first ones to take me up on my offer. Bob Long has found a strong attraction over in the Horseshoe Bend settlement and Banjy is sitting up to a widow on Wolf Creek like a kitten to an open hearth on a winter night. Old Meletone is dead, and I will take Nig with me to my home on the ranch.

We have a railroad in Coleman town now and a fine school. The little schoolmarm that you used to know down on the Red Bank is teaching in our school here.

All the boys have had their fling at her, but as a close observer, I know she is waiting for someone else. She asks about you now and then, and the other day she told me she was keeping a knife that you lost some time back.

I think you had better come home, Bill. We need you to help build our country, and incidentally make some of the wealth that was here under our noses all the time and we couldn't see. But more than we need you and more than the money you might make, you need the influence of a woman which I am sure is yours for the asking, and I will close by saying that you are the luckiest scamp of my entire acquaintance.

As ever your friend,

ROBT. H. DENMAN (The Old Hoss)

Collins folded up the letter gently and laid it upon the bar.

'Good old Bill,' he murmured. 'The best is not too good for him, and we ought to say something.'

In spite of his vehement words a softness smoothed the lines of Charlie's face. His chin quivered and a film of moisture gathered in his eyes. He turned and produced a bottle and filled two glasses, preparing to pay the strongest tribute that he knew.

The eyes of Bill's two friends met in silence. Their glasses came together above the bar with a sharp clink.

'To Bill and the girl he's riding to see,' said Collins warmly.

THE END